Queen Bee

ELIZABETH WEIGANDT

◆ FriesenPress

Suite 300 - 990 Fort St

Victoria, BC, V8V 3K2

Canada

www.friesenpress.com

ISBN

978-1-4602-9449-9 (Hardcover)

978-1-4602-9450-5 (Paperback)

978-1-4602-9451-2 (eBook)

1. JUVENILE FICTION, ANIMALS, INSECTS, SPIDERS, ETC.

Distributed to the trade by The Ingram Book Company

For Matt, who believed.

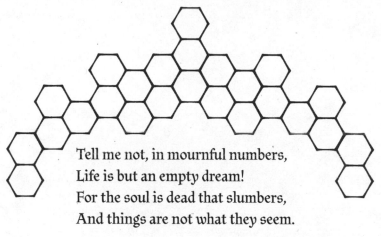

Tell me not, in mournful numbers,
Life is but an empty dream!
For the soul is dead that slumbers,
And things are not what they seem.

—from "A Psalm of Life," by
Henry Wadsworth Longfellow

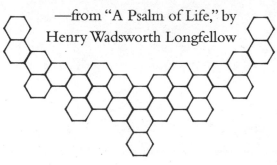

Chapter 1

The hive was already humid.

Manuka leaned down again to scoop up the puddled honey that had leaked from the massive honeycombs dangling over her head. She scraped it into her wax bucket carefully, making sure to catch every drop. Any guard who saw her wasting their precious food source would go running and report it to the Comb Warden – and from there it would surely get back to Acacia.

Clean-up duty at the top of the colony might not be her favorite assignment; she would rather be down the hall where the other worker bees were busy re-capping and repairing combs, but at least this way she could be alone with her thoughts and a safe distance away from Acacia's ever-watchful eye.

As chief attendant to the queen, Acacia's job was to fulfill all orders and maintain the hive's security. Still, with all that responsibility, she had developed an unnatural interest in Manuka.

Manuka wondered if it was because Acacia had spotted her peeping through a crack in the wall of the ward of the male drones a day earlier. As she threatened to have the guards drag Manuka away to Confinement, something about Acacia's wild stare had made Manuka wonder if she would prefer to do something much worse.

Manuka was used to being unpopular. Her ideas were odd — or what most bees considered odd, given that they were all just trying to fit in — but Acacia's animosity seemed to run deeper than that. How much deeper, Manuka couldn't tell. She was still pretty young, only a year and a half old, and like thousands of her sisters, she was just trying to get along and fulfill her duties in a world built on tradition and rules.

As she finished swiping the last of the honey into her bucket, she glanced around and, seeing no one, quickly dipped her hand in and took a mouthful. She swallowed fast but still caught the intense sweetness and the aromas (plus something else she couldn't quite identify) of at least a hundred different wildflowers from the two-mile radius they called home.

Manuka had never been outside their hive, which she was told hung high in the branches of an ancient maple tree, but she heard the world was beautiful, bright, and nearly infinite. She licked her fingers and palm furtively, making sure to clean away all the stickiness. Honey was already running short, though it was late summer, and they should have had a surplus by now. Due to a lack of rain in the spring that continued through summer, there was a scarcity of flowers and the foragers who returned each night said they had to fly farther and farther to find blossoms and collect the nectar inside them.

On top of it, many of the bees were getting sick, and the healers couldn't tell if it was due to their added exertions to find flowers or if a strange disease was spreading. In the ward just below hers, both Thistle and Sage had coughed all through the night. That morning, Manuka overheard them both protesting loudly against Captain Bergamot, their Comb Warden, whose command was that they stay in their bunks for the day so they didn't infect others.

Though it was considered a great shame to be unable to work (most bees worked proudly until their deaths), she wondered if a work-relief system could be created to allow each bee a full day of rest weekly so they could renew themselves. All that was required was a little creativity in organizing the shifts for tending to the newborns, filling the combs, wing-fanning the hive, cleaning, and so forth. Plus, maybe then the bees would live longer? She wondered what Queen Trillium would think of the idea, if she had a chance to hear it.

She might as well put the bucket on her head and proclaim *herself* queen while she was at it. She noticed another honey puddle farther down the hall and headed in its direction, smiling as Cotton's words came unbidden to her head: *Our job is orders, not ideas.*

Life would certainly be easier if she would listen to her more often.

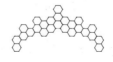

As Manuka watched the workers hoist the massive wax receptacle, now filled with honey, back up to the top of the combs, Cotton hurried in with an alarmed expression on her face.

"Manuka, come quickly," she motioned her to follow. "The queen has summoned everyone to meet in the Great Chamber immediately."

Manuka put down her bucket and followed, catching up quickly.

Like everyone in the hive, and even Manuka herself, Cotton was thinner than usual. They were down to just two rations of honey, from the usual three, per day, and Manuka noted that her friend's small frame was looking even narrower. If they didn't watch out, they'd all soon be mistaken for stick bugs instead of bees.

Due to her short stature, Cotton looked diminutive, but inside she held a tenacious spirit and a by-the-books approach to hive life. Like Manuka, most of her body was covered in a, soft velvety down. On that surface, blackish-brown and gold stripes played together over her arms, legs, abdomen and torso before culminating in the deep gold intensity of her face. On that plane, large brown eyes darted this way and that, framed by punctuating stripes before ending in a thatch of tufty brown hair she kept combed meticulously out of her eyes and away from her sensitive black antennae.

Silver gossamer wings that were folded neatly against her back brushed the wells of her knees as she ran and the tops of the smooth jet-black fins on her calves, known as pollen baskets, used for transporting nutritious pollen back to the hive.

"What's happened?" Manuka asked, wondering what could cause the queen to stop production in the middle of the day. She'd never heard of such a thing.

"Don't know," Cotton replied. "But did you hear? Thistle and Sage are dead."

"Dead? How can that be? They were alive this morning when we left."

"Captain Bergamot told me just before she sent me to get you. She said after morning feed, they both closed their eyes in their bunks and never woke up. The undertakers have already taken them outside."

"Do they know what killed them?" Manuka whispered as they both unfurled their wings and flew into one of the Down Shafts the colony used to descend throughout the hive. It was already nearly full, with almost identical bees of all ranks fluttering down to the middle level where the Great Chamber was located.

"No idea," Cotton whispered back as they arrived and exited with the others. Manuka had been to the Great Chamber only once before, on her christening, though she didn't remember it.

They walked together down the crowded main passage. It was a wide, oval-shaped tunnel made of wax, the bees' primary building material, which was also made from their main food source: honey. Manuka glanced upward and saw in the level above the faint hexagonal outlines of another Comb Ward. Not an inch of space was wasted in the hive, especially one as old as theirs that had housed many generations of bees.

"Other bees are dead too," Cotton added. "Something is going on, but no one knows what. Maybe the queen has some news, and that's why we're summoned."

"I hope so," replied Manuka. "Do you think the queen would listen if I told her my idea of having bees take breaks to conserve energy? Or, wait! What if we asked the male drones to help out? I've never even seen one of them."

"Are you crazy?" Cotton whispered. "Why are you so fascinated by them, anyway?"

"I don't know. I guess I don't understand why they have to live as outsiders. I mean, we all have the same mother. What's the big deal?"

"The deal is it's tradition, and it's not for us to question." She shook her head in disapproval as they entered the Great Chamber. "Look, we have enough on our hands and don't need anyone dragging you off to Confinement, okay? Our job is orders…"

"…not ideas," Manuka finished.

Cotton turned away in exasperation, and Manuka rolled her eyes. It was a typical response, after all. Why did she even open her mouth at all? One simple reason, she remembered ruefully: She couldn't help it.

The bees shuffled in with minimum fuss and noise, making room for one another with occasional and cordial utterances of, "Excuse me, sister." Everyone in the hive, except Acacia, was either the daughter or son of Queen Trillium. Females made up the majority and took on the various duties of hive life, whether as workers, foragers, guardians, or attendants to the queen. Male drones were much fewer and were segregated away from their sisters in the Drone Ward. Manuka looked around and noticed that, of course, none of them were present. Drones weren't allowed to leave their ward for any reason, though she couldn't figure out why.

She noticed some of the foragers still had bits of sticky yellow pollen stuck in the baskets on their arms and legs from their rush to get to the gathering. At the perimeter of the hexagonal room, the guards took their places, near the exits, in case they were suddenly needed outside to defend against a predator or wasp attack. Guards carried long carved spears made from the wood of the hive's own maple tree. Each was tipped with a piece of glittering petrified sap, known as amber, and honed to a sharp, deadly edge.

Manuka wanted one of those spears more than she wanted anything else, and she knew with one in her hand bees would finally take her seriously. They were Acacia's invention and had revolutionized hive security. Since each female honeybee, including Manuka, had a barbed stinger that would lodge permanently in an attacker if used, bees couldn't sting without being killed themselves. The spears fixed this problem and made each bee wielding one a formidable threat.

To earn a spear, a bee would first have to serve as a worker, then as a forager, before training to become a guard. Many foragers didn't even survive the threats of the outside world so those that had made it all the way to becoming guards held especially coveted and respected roles in hive life.

Manuka reminded herself she still had a chance to wield a spear of her own one day. The poor, stingerless male drones didn't. Their only contribution was manufacturing the spears – an effort sanctioned and supervised by Acacia herself.

Manuka watched as Acacia and the second attendant, Laurel, filed in, each taking a place on the dais. Acacia's whole story was unknown. The rumor went she had come to Queen Trillium's hive as a lost bee. Normally, she would have been turned away, but Acacia carried an amber spear, something the bees had never heard of or seen before. She was taken to Queen Trillium, who welcomed her in exchange for her knowledge of making and using the spears for defense against attacking wasps.

Once the wasps were neutralized, Acacia was appointed chief attendant. Ever since, the drones made the spears, the guards used them, and their hive had become relatively safe.

Because the wasps could attack again at any time, Manuka wondered why all the bees weren't similarly armed for defense. The only bee in the hive who didn't need a spear was Queen Trillium, who had a smooth, barbless stinger, allowing her to defend herself repeatedly without ever risking injury.

A group of bees stationed themselves above in evenly spaced alcoves and were already furiously fanning their wings to keep air circulating in the Great Chamber.

Manuka wondered what their view was like from up there but then Acacia's toneless voice boomed from the center of the queen's dais, shocking her back to reality.

"Attention, sisters," she repeated and paused as her voice echoed throughout the room, making use of its perfect acoustics. "Shortly, you will all be able to return to your tasks, but for now Queen Trillium has an announcement that pertains to every bee in the colony."

"If it's every bee in the colony, why aren't the drones here?" Manuka whispered in Cotton's ear. She jumped a foot in shock at someone speaking during an official gathering and stamped on Manuka's foot to quiet her.

"Ouch!" Manuka gasped, to which Cotton raised a finger, giving her the death stare. Other bees tilted their antennae slightly in their direction, wondering at the cause of the commotion.

A hush fell over the crowd as the queen went to her dais. She wore an elaborate golden crown made of wax hexagons and a robe of woven purple coneflower petals. She stood at least a head taller than other bees – another trait related to her special breeding as a queen.

"Greetings, my children. It has come to my attention that we don't have enough honey to last the rest of the summer, let alone the fall and winter. Each day our foragers return with less and less nectar, and there seem to be even fewer flowers than we expected for this time of year."

Gasps erupted throughout the hall accompanied by a nervous fluttering of wings. Ever since the start of summer, just two months prior, bees had been working overtime to ensure the hive would have enough honey. There had been whispers that it would be tough to fill all the honeycombs, but everyone buckled down, as bees do, to ensure they would achieve their goal. The reality of what the queen's pronouncement meant, that they would all likely die before winter, was unthinkable.

"Quiet, ladies, we're going to assign double shifts to our current foragers, and some of you workers will learn to forage sooner than intended. Plus, there's more you should hear." The queen smoothed her gown and seemed to collect herself. "As you have no doubt seen and heard, there is a sickness spreading throughout the hive. My attendants, the healers, and I still don't know its cause, and we ask that if you see anyone coughing or unwell that you notify your Comb Warden immediately. The best we can do is quarantine those bees who exhibit symptoms while we deal with this other threat of scarcity."

The bees murmured their agreement and waited obediently for the queen to continue.

"What about the *drones*?" Manuka shouted at the top of her lungs. More gasps and thousands of heads immediately turned, staring in her direction.

"Excuse me? Who is that?" asked the queen, raising a hand over her eyes and squinting to find the voice in the sea of faces.

"It's *Manuka*!" Manuka shouted, glancing sideways at Cotton, who had already covered her face in shame.

"Manuka…" the queen hesitated, clearly perplexed, then she added, "Please come forward."

"Well, you heard her, big mouth. Get up there!" Cotton said, shoving her.

Manuka made her way through the crowd, which parted easily enough given that no one wanted to be associated with her, and prayed that the queen might at least be entertained by her idea enough to prevent Acacia from throwing her in Confinement. However, once she got to the dais and saw the frowns on everyone's faces, including the queen's, she felt her stomach drop.

"Please come here, my dear," said the queen, gesturing her forward. "Let's hear what you have to say."

Manuka's legs trembled, but she still did as commanded and took the steps upward to the dais. The queen took her hand and brought her forward. Manuka marveled at the beauty of her older, much wiser face, as it looked down, not unkindly, on her own. The queen's gaze seemed to hold a sadness, as if something had been lost, but it evaporated, replaced instantly by congeniality, making her wonder if she had seen it at all.

The queen pointed her forward. "Now, please tell everyone what you wanted to say."

Manuka swallowed hard and glanced over at Acacia, whose black eyes glared malignantly at her as she stood with her fingers curling around her own spear. Acacia stood nearly as tall and elegant as the queen and wore a long robe of brilliant green spearmint leaves. The queen's second attendant, Laurel, stood at Acacia's left and slightly behind. She was smaller and rotund, wearing a plain robe of white daisy petals. Her antennae twitched nervously from side to side as she watched Manuka. Instead of a spear, she grasped a scroll of resin to her chest. It was undoubtedly the ledger of the hive's honey and pollen stores, as Laurel was in charge of production.

"I wanted to say, what about the male drones?" Manuka said. "They don't really do anything. Can't we send them out to forage? I mean, their lives are at stake too."

The queen raised her dark eyebrows. "Well, that is an idea. But the drones are forbidden from interacting with the rest of the hive. They wouldn't be able to go up to the honeycombs to deposit their nectar and pollen, even if they were able to find any."

"How come?" asked Manuka as more shocked gasps rippled throughout the chamber at the audacity of a worker questioning the queen. "I mean, why is that?"

The queen smiled patiently. "It's always been that way. It's tradition."

"But you can change that, right? You make the rules. Just send them out with a few foragers who can teach them the ropes. What do we have to lose?" she threw in, figuring that if she was going to be punished anyway, she might as well go all the way.

"Thank you, Manuka. I'll think about it," said the queen, smiling in amusement. "I do remember when I named you," she added with a wink and gestured her to the side and continued her address. "We can *all* thank Manuka for her desire to help," she said with a sidelong glance at Acacia, who never stopped glowering.

Manuka stepped away and stood awkwardly to the side by herself as the queen finished her speech, marveling at the poise she displayed in addressing the thousands of bees before her. She peered into the crowd, which all seemed to meld together from her vantage point, and tried to find Cotton, who she was sure was seething and preparing choice words for her later in the Ward.

Manuka tried to think of a way to explain why she had spoken out the way she had, but a single clear reason wouldn't come. Instead, she wondered why having an idea at all had to be such an outrage. Extreme problems called for new solutions, right? Sadly, she realized she was truly the only one who thought so and felt the sting of tears at the corners of her eyes. She forced herself to stare at the ground, trying not to think about what would be coming her way next for speaking out so brashly, and of all bees, to Queen Trillium.

Manuka flew back to her Ward alone. No bee would come near her, although she could feel their eyes and hear their whispers all around her. When she arrived, she headed straight for her bunk and found Cotton waiting with her arms crossed.

"Well, I hope you're satisfied," she said. "If people thought you were strange before, now they're convinced you are nuts."

"But I'm not," Manuka replied and hopped up into her bed without looking at her friend, folding her wings delicately behind her. Her stomach grumbled again, making her feel more aggravated. "It was a good idea, and I still stand by it." She lay down flat in her bed and closed her eyes, hoping Cotton would get the hint and just go away. It didn't work.

"Manuka…" Cotton began and then paused as she sought the right words. "I just think you would be a lot happier and have more friends if you let others figure things out and focused on doing your work and fitting in."

"I have a question for you." Manuka sat up, swinging her legs over the side of her bed and facing down. "If we're all sisters, we're basically all the same, right?"

"I suppose…" Cotton said.

"And if we're all sisters, and we all have the same mother and were born from the same combs, then that means there's no difference between the value of my ideas and the value of your ideas or the value of the queen's attendants."

"Just can't keep a cork in it, can you?" called out Captain Bergamot as she stalked toward them.

Manuka held her reply, not wanting to anger Bergamot. Cotton also fell silent, recoiling slightly, as if she was anticipating what was coming next.

"That was quite a display, even for you," Captain Bergamot continued. Across her chest, she wore a special braided grass sash, signifying her rank as Comb Warden. "Also, I can report, Acacia was *not* pleased."

"When is she ever?" Manuka murmured, falling back in her bunk.

"What was that?" Captain Bergamot asked.

"Nothing," Manuka mumbled.

"Manuka, I don't care if you think you're special, so special that you can just bellow out whatever you want in a formal assembly, embarrassing this ward with your effrontery to the queen. You were very lucky she was amused by your thoughtlessness. I, however, was not, and you can look forward to double duty tomorrow in the Refuse Ward to think about your actions."

Manuka groaned. Only once before had she been required to serve a day in the Refuse Ward, and she had hoped never to return. It was a nasty place, where the bees sorted and ejected their garbage from the hive. Double duty meant a 24-hour shift with almost no rest, and afterward, she would be so exhausted, she wouldn't be able to think at all — a state called minormind — which most bees cherished for its thoughtlessness and mental peace. Manuka shuddered, preferring the heady whirl of her own lively thoughts to the dead space of total fatigue.

"Cotton will join you," Captain Bergamot added as an afterthought.

"What? But I didn't do anything," Cotton protested.

"Well, maybe she'll think twice next time. She clearly doesn't care about herself. I guess now we'll see if she cares about you. Report tomorrow at first light." Captain Bergamot turned on her heel and headed for her bunk at the far end of the Comb Ward, muttering something about being a glorified babysitter.

Manuka looked down at Cotton and saw her clenching her hands and grinding her jaw. "I'm sorry," she said, hoping Cotton would believe her.

"Whatever," Cotton replied and went into her bunk and out of Manuka's sight. They didn't speak for the rest of the night.

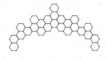

The next morning, as Manuka and Cotton were getting ready, they overheard a hacking cough coming from the far end of the comb. Together, they headed in its direction and found it belonged to Captain Bergamot, who was still in bed.

"Stay away," she said hoarsely, covering her mouth through more coughs as she lay under her sheep's ear coverlet. "Get on with your work for the day, girls, all of you. I've called for a healer." Another coughing bout racked her, and she gasped for air. Manuka, Cotton, and the other bees backed away in alarm.

Two healers appeared, carrying between them a stretcher. "Nothing to see here, ladies," one said, waving them away. "Off to your daily duties." Manuka noticed that both of them were wild-eyed and clearly flustered as they bent over Bergamot, checking her vital signs and whispering to each other.

How many more have they had to visit this morning? Manuka wondered.

"Come on," Cotton said to Manuka. "Let's let them work. Feel better, Captain Bergamot. We'll see you later today," she threw in before they turned away.

Captain Bergamot didn't respond. Her eyes were closed and her color was pale. Manuka wondered what she would look like when they got back, if she was still there at all.

Chapter 2

Later, as they descended on the Down Shaft toward the Refuse Ward at the far bottom of the hive, Manuka said, "This is getting really scary."

Cotton nodded. "There's nothing we can do about it, though. The healers will find the cause sooner or later."

"What if they don't?" Manuka asked, not being able to help it.

Cotton gave an exasperated sigh. "Manuka, it's not for us to worry about. Why can't you just let things go?"

"I don't know," Manuka murmured as they finally landed at the bottom, wondering for the thousandth time what it was that made her so different from other bees. Together, they proceeded down another oval corridor, as the stench of the hive's garbage grew stronger. "I just can't stop my mind from buzzing all the time. I have a million questions, and they all want to be answered. When other bees are working at their tasks, I'm working too, but in my head… I've tried to stop, but I can't. It seems like even minormind doesn't work on me."

"I can't say I understand, but I know you've been this way since we were born," Cotton said, glancing at her. Her soft brown eyes carried a worried expression. "I just wish you would exercise a little more control over it, that's all."

Manuka nodded. "I'll try to do better. I really am sorry for dragging you into this. You're my only friend, Cotton," she added with a twinge of desperation.

"I know," Cotton said as they arrived at the heavy-duty wax doors that sectioned off the Refuse Ward. Both of them covered their noses at the smell, and inside, they could hear the many pulleys and shouts of the bees that manned them. "Guess we might as well get this over with," Cotton said and rapped hard, notifying the workers inside they had arrived.

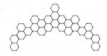

After twelve hours, they were finally allowed a short break and a chance to eat. Both Manuka and Cotton slumped in a corner away from the others to sip their respective honey rations, handed to them in small, edible wax cups.

"I don't know if I've ever been this tired," Cotton said. "How does the warden handle working down here day after day? The stench alone would drive you crazy."

"We all have our talents," Manuka said with a grin, taking a gulp of honey.

"I guess," Cotton laughed. Her eyes crinkled, making the stripes on either side of her face contract slightly. She took a sip of honey.

After her first swallow, Manuka sniffed her honey. "Do you notice a weird aftertaste?"

"No, I don't think so," Cotton said, looking down at her cup with a puzzled look on her face.

"Try it again, but this time, smell it first."

Cotton did as she was asked, and then looked at Manuka quizzically.

"Notice anything?" Manuka asked. "Like a rotten taste?"

"Honey doesn't rot. It lasts forever." Cotton said.

"Yes, but something's wrong with this. It doesn't smell clean, like new flowers, like it normally does."

"You're crazy," Cotton said, rolling her eyes and taking another sip, but this time wrinkling her nose afterward.

"I'm not," Manuka said with conviction. "What if this is what's making everyone sick?"

"Even if it were, what can we do about it? This is all the honey we have. If we don't eat this, we'll starve."

"You say I don't make sense, but that doesn't make sense either," Manuka said. "What if we stopped eating the honey and just ate the pollen? That's got more protein in it anyway."

"The pollen isn't as plentiful, and you know it. Besides, it's for the queen and her attendants. If the whole hive ate it, we'd only have enough for a few days, at the most."

Cotton had a point. Regular bees needed the calorie-rich honey to keep up with the pace of work they set for themselves. Manuka felt her brain come alive with all the questions and possible solutions this presented, one feeding into another and another.

Recognizing what was happening, Cotton's voice took on an alarmed tone. "Don't you get started," she said. "We've got another twelve hours of this to get through, and I don't want another twelve heaped on top of it."

"But what if I'm right?" Manuka asked.

"Break's over! Everyone back to work!" the Refuse Warden bellowed to the group.

Cotton thought about it, pursing her lips, and looked intently at Manuka. "Can't do anything about it now. Just… try thinking it over while you work before blurting out any half-baked ideas. We can talk about it after, okay?"

Manuka knew she didn't have much choice. "Deal," she said.

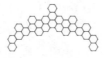

When they finally straggled into their Comb Ward, instead of finding all the bees sleeping quietly in their beds, they found the group in a frantic twitter, busily gossiping in the middle of the room.

"What's going on?" Manuka said to Cotton as they dropped their things.

"Did you hear?" Sweetpea said, coming over. "Captain Bergamot is dead, and the queen is sick now too."

"What?" Manuka said as she and Cotton exchanged looks of alarm. Manuka quickly pulled her aside. "Cotton, we have to tell someone."

"Tell who what?" Cotton asked. "About the honey? That's just a theory."

"Well, at least I have one," Manuka snapped. "I did as you said, and I thought about it the rest of the day. How couldn't it be the honey? We're all eating it, and something isn't right with it. I bet I'm not the only one who's noticed, just the only one who *said* something."

Cotton recoiled as if slapped. "Fine, make a fool out of yourself. Just don't come running to me when they drag you away for insubordination."

Manuka went to the Up Shaft, took it to the middle level, and ran through the Great Chamber toward the entrance to the queen's living quarters, which was at the back of the room, to the right of the dais. When she arrived, two guards sporting dark brown bark armor and amber spears blocked her path.

"I have to see the queen!" she shouted. "Something is wrong with the honey. It's making everyone sick!"

"Back to your Ward, troublemaker!" said one of the guards, who pushed her away, causing Manuka to fall on the ground.

At that moment, Laurel waddled out with an exasperated look on her face. She wore a simple robe of dandelion leaves, and her antennae were already twitching excitedly in her thatch of brown hair. "Move out of the way, you silly girl," she said as she passed.

"I'm telling you! The honey is poisoned. Can't you smell it or taste it?" Both guards exchanged questioning glances, and Laurel stopped, turning around to listen. "We need to get rid of it or everyone is going to die," Manuka continued.

"What's all this noise?" Acacia said hotly as she stormed out of the queen's quarters, wearing a robe of yellow daisy petals. "*You*," she hissed, her black eyes narrowing. "Get her out of here, now. The last thing the queen needs is to be disturbed again by this *freak*."

Suddenly, Cotton ran up and joined Manuka's side. "Wait! I think she may be right. There *is* something strange about the honey."

"I see," Acacia replied, exchanging a meaningful glance with Laurel, who seemed to be holding her breath. "Take them both then." She nodded to the guards, who pinned both Manuka's and Cotton's arms painfully behind their backs. "We're not tolerating troublemakers or those intent on hogging the queen's attention, no matter *who* they think they are. Put them in Confinement until I can deal with them."

Chapter 3

Laurel padded as quietly as she could down the passage-way that led to Acacia's private chambers. Given that it was the middle of the night, and most of the bees were asleep in their beds, she didn't expect to be seen, but she still felt nervous. Arriving at Acacia's door, she tapped as quietly as she could with a chubby brown fist and tried to shoo away the butterflies once and for all. The door swung open silently, and she met Acacia's black, bottomless stare. It was then she wondered if her anxiety had more to do with her present company than the circumstances of their visit.

"Come in, won't you?" Acacia murmured and stepped aside so Laurel could enter. Her dressing gown of gold petunia petals edged in white caterpillar silk rustled slightly. Laurel saw that the lower part of her neck was exposed, and that it was inky black also, like her face, antennae, and hair. Most bees' faces were golden, with dark brown eyes and then black and gold stripes on their foreheads, torsos, and abdomens; Acacia, however, was rumored to be jet black from head to toe, an exceptionally rare trait.

As she entered, Laurel noted that Acacia's chamber was one room, like her own, but was outfitted much more luxuriously. Above them, an ornate chandelier of wax candles flickered. The faceted crystals on its arms were a honey-colored brown, but Laurel knew they weren't made of honey but of rare amber and had been fashioned by the same male drones who resided in the forbidden Drone Ward and made the spears used by their guards to defend the hive.

"Like it?" Acacia said, following her gaze. "I thought the room needed a little extra something."

Laurel noted that Acacia had collected several extra somethings. A freshly-woven coverlet of sheep's ear leaves lay on her bed, and a lush rug of cool green moss was beneath their feet. In the far corner, an ornate maple table stood with two matching chairs. On top of it was a carved wax bowl of dew with a single miniature rose floating in its center. Laurel licked her lips as she caught the scent of its sweet nectar and realized she had been too busy to have Evening Meal.

"Would you care for some?" Acacia offered. "It was brought in this afternoon."

But Laurel had other pressing things on her mind besides food. "Why is the queen sick?" she asked pointedly.

"I have no idea," Acacia replied smoothly, never breaking her gaze. "You might ask one of her minor attendants."

"But the queen only eats pollen. Who would have given her honey?"

Acacia held her answer for a beat. "Again, this is a question for someone else," she replied.

Laurel sighed. "You realize if she dies, we're in real trouble. We need more workers for honey production, and there is no one but her to breed them."

Acacia laughed. "I thought you wanted to swarm to another location. Isn't that what you told me a month ago, when we decided to poison the honey?"

"Yes, finding a new home is imperative, but how can we organize a swarm if we don't have a queen to lead it? You know what will happen without her; the bees will scatter themselves to the wind without her scent to guide them. We'll lose everything."

"Look, you wanted a swarm, and ultimately, you'll get one…"

"But…"

"I'll find a way to make sure she only has pollen from now on. She'll recover, and then we can continue with Plan A, getting her to agree to a swarm due to both of our pressing concerns: the flower drought and the pervading sickness. Both will finally force her to take action, and we'll have a new home before you know it."

"What about Manuka and Cotton? They seem to know about the honey."

Acacia smiled, her white teeth standing out against her face. "Don't worry about them. They are about to become very busy little bees indeed."

Laurel tried to conceal her shudder. "Still, if someone tells the queen that they've been confined, she might be upset, or worse, want to hear what they have to say."

"I'm not concerned," Acacia replied casually as she went to one of her chairs and seated herself (quite regally, Laurel thought).

"Do you ever wonder if she knows?" Laurel asked.

"If who knows?" Acacia answered as she twirled the rose in its bowl.

"Manuka. The legend and all."

Acacia went very still, and her opaque eyes flicked back to Laurel. "It's just a name," she said. Laurel felt another chill. Acacia looked down and noticed one of her black legs had escaped her robe. Impatiently, she threw the fabric over herself. "The queen is senile and has been for some time. Why else has she ignored your warnings about the flower drought?"

"I'm not sure I would say she's senile, just stubborn. This hive has been in her family for ten generations. Her ancestors survived a few flower droughts whenever rain was scarce, plus the Wasp War, so she believes we can survive this too."

"But she's wrong."

"I believe she is, yes. I've had scouts mapping the flowers for two years now. There just aren't enough. If we moved farther away…"

"Yes, I know," Acacia said brusquely. "My point is that we need to act, and we need to stick with our plan. That should be our focus, not whatever ridiculous name the queen decided to give to a single *worthless* bee."

Laurel nodded. "I know you're right... I just didn't think this many bees would die, and I didn't think that the poisoned honey would be discovered so soon."

"Nothing's been discovered. Besides, bees die all the time, and you know that. We must put the greater good first," Acacia said, standing. She gestured toward the door, indicating that their meeting was at an end. "Let's talk again before the moon sets tomorrow night. In the meantime, leave the queen, Manuka, and Cotton to me."

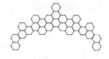

"Cotton, please say something," Manuka said from across their cell. "I know you're awake."

It was nearly morning, and Cotton was still lying on her back on the dingy bunk opposite Manuka's with her eyes closed. She had not responded to any of Manuka's entreaties, and her mouth was pressed into a thin line under a determined frown.

"Cotton, I'm sorry. I didn't think you would follow me to the queen's..." Cotton flipped angrily on her side, away from her, and refolded her wings in a huff over her skinny dark legs. "But I want to thank you for standing by me, anyway," she finished.

Manuka sighed and decided to let her alone. She reclined back in her own creaky bunk and looked up at the ceiling of the Confinement Ward. Their cell was fortified by dense twig bars secured in place by a sturdy mixture of wax and resin. It was very dark, and a single candle, which sat in a corner just outside their cell, faintly lit their section of the Ward, casting more shadows than light.

About an hour later, Manuka woke from her doze to the stomping sound of many feet approaching. "Quick, Cotton. Wake up!" she said, nudging her friend. Cotton opened her eyes, and together, they stood to see who was coming.

Acacia appeared, followed by six armored guards carrying spears. The first, walking immediately behind her, was Coriander, Acacia's vicious whip-thin personal guard, who was known for executing all of Acacia's commands to the letter.

"Hello, girls," Acacia purred. "You have been given a new assignment, by order of the queen."

"Please tell the queen we are very sorry," Cotton said. "We never intended to cause her or her attendants any inconvenience…"

"Quiet!" Acacia snapped, her eyes flaring. "And you'll stay that way unless you want me to change my mind and choose a more severe punishment for your treason. Take them."

The guards pulled them out of the cell.

"Treason?" Manuka said as her hands were tightly bound behind her. "We're worried about the hive…"

Coriander stepped forward and slapped her hard across the face. Manuka felt her teeth rattle inside her stinging cheek. Whatever she had been planning to say flew out of her head.

"That's better," Acacia said, smiling. "Let's go."

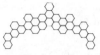

Manuka and Cotton were led out of the Confinement Ward with their hands tied with grass twine behind their backs and under their wings. After descending down a set a stairs, they reached a small door marked "Restricted" that Acacia unlocked with a key she withdrew from her robe. Once through, they entered a room where they were confronted by two huge brown wasps, roaring in towering twig cages and struggling fiercely against bonds of their own.

"We need to reinforce the right side of Number Two's cage again. She already knocked out one of her bars," Coriander pointed out to Acacia. Manuka noted that, though she didn't carry a spear and looked like a regular worker bee, she carried a dagger made of amber in a belt around her waist.

"Deal with it later," Acacia replied. "Now, get the prisoners close enough in front of them so they can get their scents."

"What are you going to do with us?" Manuka asked, hearing her own voice quaver with terror, as the guards pushed them forward in front of each of the cages.

"You'll see," Acacia said.

Manuka saw that each wasp was held in place by a collar and thick twine rope, though that didn't stop them from clawing ferociously between the bars. Cotton screamed, trying to back away, but was held firmly in place just out of reach. She whimpered in fright as both wasps leaned forward and snuffled their scents, spreading apart razor-sharp mandibles as they did so.

"That should do it," Acacia said, walking over to a large door marked exit and opening it as wide as possible, letting in the cool pre-dawn air. "Bring them here." The guards obeyed and dragged both bees over, positioning them at the opening, where they could peer into the dark mists below. "Now listen closely," she said from her place at the door's side. "You have two choices: remain here when we release the wasps, or fly out now and try to escape on your own."

"Why are you doing this to us?" Manuka asked. "What did we ever do to you?"

"Ask another question and you can take your chances in here for all I care," she answered.

"We'll fly," Cotton volunteered, blinking back tears.

"Good choice," Acacia said, and the guards edged them forward so they now teetered over the door's rim.

"Wait! Aren't you going to untie us first?" Manuka asked.

"Why would we do that?" Acacia replied and nodded to Coriander, who roughly shoved them into the darkness below.

Manuka flapped her wings furiously, trying to stabilize herself, but it was very awkward with her arms tied behind her back. Instead, she did a mixture of fluttering and falling as she narrowly dodged larger tree branches on her way down and got smacked in the face more than once by flat maple leaves.

Just when she thought she might have the hang of it, she slammed into a low, errant branch and was knocked nearly senseless. She fell to the grass several feet below in a daze and lay with her face in the moist earth, feeling somewhat fortunate she hadn't crushed a wing. She sat up on her knees and tried to get her bearings, knowing she had to find Cotton before the wasps did.

She shimmied backward, first sitting on top of her bound wrists, then moving them under her legs and over her feet so they were now clasped in front of her. She used her sharp incisors to gnaw away the grass binding and, in seconds, she was free and standing up.

"Cotton!" she said as loudly as she dared and began picking her way through the growth, hoping not to run into anything more formidable than a wasp.

As she walked, the light of dawn began to peek through the blades of grass. The air smelled of mud and decomposing leaves. Behind her she heard a rustle, "Cotton?" she said hopefully, turning around. No reply and she couldn't see anything moving. *Whatever that is, it's not Cotton.* She turned, walking faster and continued calling until she finally heard a faint "Here…" in the brush. She ran forward and found her friend flailing face down, wings buzzing, in a puddle of mud, with her arms still tied behind her.

"Here, let me help you," she said, rushing forward. She clipped away Cotton's bindings with her teeth, and she was soon free. "We have to fly fast before those wasps find us or something else does."

"Where can we go?" Cotton replied, but then pricked her ears up as they both heard the approaching wup-wup-wup sound of large wings beating furiously.

"I don't know. But we don't have time to figure it out now. They know where we are. Take my hand and fly as fast as you can!"

Cotton did so, and together, they leapt into the air, breaking through the grass barrier and into the soft pink light of dawn. The wasps were upon them immediately, swiveling around them on either side, roaring with claws extended. "Go!" Manuka shouted and beat her wings frantically, pulling Cotton straight upward.

As they gained air and then darted forward, the world swam before Manuka's eyes. She had never anticipated it would be so immense, so full of color, smells, and shapes. Still, she didn't have time to appreciate any of it, and instead, focused on the horizon for balance, flying as fast as their wings would take them. The wasps picked up speed as well, and she could hear their frustrated shrieks close behind.

After a mile or so, both bees were gasping for air, and Manuka knew they wouldn't be able to last much longer. She glanced behind her briefly and saw both wasps were keeping pace with determined savagery.

"What if we dove into that clump of bushes up ahead?" panted Cotton. "Maybe we can lose them that way?"

Manuka nodded, and they descended into a thicket. The wasps followed, dodging branches and leaves. Soon they came upon a small clearing, and suddenly, they heard a female's husky voice shout from above, "Get 'em!" and something large, with bright yellow stripes, came plummeting out of the sky, knocking one of the wasps to the ground.

More black and yellow bodies, shouting war cries, plunged stingers first, and soon mobbed the remaining wasp, balling around it in a mass. In minutes, both creatures lay still and lifeless on the grass.

Manuka and Cotton touched down on the leaves of a nearby sapling and stared in awe as the insects, who appeared to be giant, furry bees, hovered around them, their buzzing wings keeping their massive bodies curiously aloft. Before long, one of the largest bees, whom they recognized as the first to attack the wasps, set down in front of them. She stood with her hands planted on either side of her big belly and grimly surveyed the two exhausted bees before her. A huge ruff of black-and-yellow-striped fur covered her chest, shoulders, and neck, making her look like she was ready for the coldest winter, though it was high summer.

"What brings you to Bombas Grove?" she said.

Chapter 4

M anuka and Cotton looked at one another in hesitation. Should they tell this formidable bee about their troubles or keep it to themselves? Seeing the decision take shape on her friend's face, Cotton began shaking her head in protest, but it was too late.

"We've been banished from our hive," Manuka said, and out of the corner of her eye, saw Cotton turn away in shame.

"Banished? And how did those two end up chasing you?" the large bee said, pointing at the bodies of the wasps.

"It's kind of a long story," Manuka replied.

"Is it? Well, you better make it a short one because I don't have time to dillydally around. The flowers are waiting. Or what little of them are left."

"We're very sorry to have troubled you, Miss… Um…" Cotton interjected.

"It's Mustard," said the bee, slightly puffing her chest.

"I see… Well, Mustard, we do appreciate your, and everyone's, bravery in saving us from the wasps." Cotton gestured to the entire group, which was still watching them with interest. "If not for you, we would be dead now. We'll leave you to the day and wish you the greatest success in your foraging."

"Hold up a second there," Mustard replied, raising a hand and curling her antennae forward. "I don't take to being brushed off, and I don't appreciate two banished bees leading a couple of wasps into our grove and then trying to waltz off without explanation. Now, you either give me some answers or you'll find yourselves in a worse mess." The other bees nodded in approval, their chins bobbing into their furry collars.

"Okay, I'll try," Manuka said. "Something is wrong with our hive's honey, and our sisters have been getting sick and dying from it. The queen herself is sick now. We tried to tell her what's going on, but her chief attendant kicked us out and sent the wasps after us."

"How could she send wasps after you?"

"She had them caged up inside the hive."

The other bees began whispering among themselves.

Mustard eyed them skeptically. "Are you sure you're not telling me a story to cover up the real reason you were banished? No one keeps wasps."

"Well, Acacia does, as crazy as it sounds," Manuka replied. "She had them tied up in cages inside our hive. I don't know how she did it, but it's a fact."

"She's telling the truth," Cotton volunteered. "I would think it was a lie too, if I hadn't seen them myself."

Mustard eyed them closely. "This sounds like one nasty bee," she said.

"That's an understatement," Cotton replied.

Mustard paused as she considered what to do next. "What are your names?"

"Manuka and Cotton," Manuka answered.

Mustard gave a start and blinked. "Did you say *Manuka*?" The other bees looked equally surprised.

Puzzled, Manuka replied. "Yes, that's my name. Is there something wrong with it?"

"Nothing, unless your queen has the strange habit of naming lowly workers after sacred bee legends."

"What do you mean?" Manuka asked.

Mustard gave an exasperated huff. "We don't have time for this. You probably know, there's a flower scarcity and the sun shows we're getting into morning. If we don't get moving, the day's nectar will be gone."

"Okay, does that mean we're free to go?" Cotton asked.

"Yes, yes. Free to go. On your way. But no bringing wasps back here again."

"We won't," said Manuka, wishing she could get Mustard to tell her why her name had surprised her so. She turned to face Cotton and saw that she had slumped against the trunk of the sapling. "Are you okay?" she asked.

"Just started feeling dizzy all of a sudden," Cotton replied. "Haven't eaten since yesterday."

Manuka felt her own belly rumble in agreement. They both needed food quickly, or they wouldn't be able to fly at all. She turned to Mustard, who was just getting ready to take to the air. "Wait! Do you happen to know if any flowers are nearby? My friend needs food."

Mustard groaned and turned back around. She saw Cotton's state and threw her hands up in the air. "See that rosebush over there? That's where we live. Follow me."

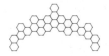

They flew as a group toward the bush, which was nearly as wide as it was tall and held only a couple wilting pink flowers on branches that should be have been filled with color. Manuka wondered where the furry bees' hive could be and searched the tight density of its green foliage. Was it at the very top or somewhere in the middle? She thought they might crash into it, but then Mustard dove sharply, and together, they landed on the ground.

"Come on," Mustard said as she strode under its canopy.

Manuka and Cotton followed her lead, picking their way through dead growth. Soon they arrived at a clear patch of ground at the base of the bush, where a small opening had been dug in the ground. A mass of bees was bustling in and out of its entrance.

"You didn't build your hive up high in the branches?" Cotton asked.

Mustard laughed. "Why would we when there are rabbits who can dig perfectly nice burrows that make even better hives? Oh, I forgot, you honeybees prefer the dizzying heights, where you can fall to your deaths. Oh well, no one's perfect. Wait here." She went into the hive's entrance, leaving them standing awkwardly to the side of the entryway.

"What if we can't find any flowers to feed ourselves?" Cotton said as she sat down wearily.

Manuka knelt in front of her and placed a hand on her shoulder. "I'll think of something," she said. "Maybe Mustard can point us in the right direction. She seems okay."

"Yeah. I just don't want to make her mad again," she whispered as she spotted Mustard return over Manuka's shoulder.

"This ought to do the trick," Mustard said, setting down a large acorn cap filled to the brim with thick, golden honey. "Well, go ahead," she added impatiently. "Eat."

They drank the sweet honey, which had an almost grassy taste, passing it back and forth between them, and felt better immediately.

"Good, good." Mustard nodded. "Now, if you'll excuse me…" She made as if to go.

"Wait!" Manuka said, standing. "I'm sorry. I know we've been a lot of trouble for you today, but we don't have anywhere to go. Could you point us in the direction of some flowers? Then we'll be out of your way."

Mustard put her hands back on her hips and cocked her head to the side in thought. "Tell you what. You two come and forage for me today, and I'll give you a couple of bunks in our hive tonight. Sound good?"

"Yes! Are you sure it's all right?" Manuka said.

"It's fine. I'm shorthanded, and we bumblebees aren't nearly as snobby as you honeybees. And if someone gets their nose out of joint, they can come see me." She thumbed her chest. "Now, you ready to fly or what? No time to lose."

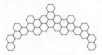

Trees slowly passed below Manuka and Cotton as they flew on either side of Mustard in the direction of a small recently bloomed clover patch she said was about a mile away.

"What's all the blue stuff on the ground?" Cotton shouted to Mustard over the din of their flapping wings and the rushing wind.

"What?" Mustard shouted back.

"The blue stuff! Why is that part of the earth the same color as the sky?" she said, pointing in the direction of a giant sparkling blue ring that circled the land before breaking and ending at more land on the other side.

"That's water!" Mustard laughed. "Didn't you know we're on an island? That's the lake!"

"What's an island?" Manuka shouted.

Mustard rolled her eyes. "It means our part of the land is surrounded by water. Haven't either of you ever been out of your hive?"

They both shook their heads.

"We didn't know there were other kinds of bees, either!" Manuka said.

"Never heard of the bumblebees! Well, I can't say I'm surprised. Your kind tends to keep to themselves, and we're fewer anyway. But what we lack in numbers, we certainly make up for in spirit!" She laughed.

Manuka smiled and then made the mistake of look-ing straight down at the rushing green landscape beneath them. It was made up of shrubs, trees, and an occasional straight grayish-brown line with what looked like odd boxy shapes trundling along at speeds sometimes faster than hers. Her stomach did a sickening flip, and she felt herself lose altitude.

"Hold up there!" Mustard said, dropping down to stay level with her. "Pick up the pace a bit! That's it!"

Manuka did as she asked and said, "How do you not feel sick all the time?"

"Easy. Don't get distracted by the scenery! See, there's the clover up ahead – that little patch of white stuff. Stay focused on that, and you'll be fine!"

Manuka did as she said and felt her stomach settle a bit. Then she remembered what she really wanted to know. "Earlier, you were surprised by my name! Why?"

Mustard glanced at her sideways, her light brown eyes reflecting the trace of a secret. "Let's just say it's very unique. You'll find out why back at the hive tonight!"

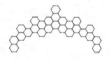

Manuka and Cotton tried to follow Mustard's foraging advice, but it wasn't easy.

It was tricky balancing on top of each clover blossom. (They had a tendency to list to the side under their weight, causing the bees to slip off.) Also, gripping the blossom just right to get the nectar without spilling it everywhere proved equally hard.

And that was nothing compared to trying to get along with the other insects, who were even more aggressive than usual due to the scarcity of flowers.

First, some bumblebees in Mustard's outfit yelled at Manuka for not waiting her turn for a particularly large and luscious yellow daisy situated just outside the clover field.

Then, Cotton missed her landing on a clover and accidentally fell on the back of a strange nearby insect with massive flat wings that were elaborately patterned with black, orange, and yellow stripes.

"I'm so sorry, ma'am!" she spluttered, hopping off and scrambling onto the next flower.

"Ma'am? *I* am the monarch of the skies," the insect replied haughtily, standing to her full height and fanning her huge wings so they blocked out the sun. "Get out of here before I knock you to the ground for the centipedes to find you!"

Cotton scrambled away, and Manuka joined her. "I think there's another grouping over there that isn't as crowded. Let's try that, okay?"

Cotton nodded sadly. "This is the worst day ever," she said, wiping away a tear.

"I know," Manuka agreed. "But maybe it'll get better. We just have to keep going. At least we made a friend and found a place to stay, right?"

"Ahem," a strange voice said behind them.

They turned around and found a honeybee attempting to stand casually, while still balancing precariously on a clover.

"Ahem," the bee repeated, placing one hand gallantly over a gold and black striped breast. "Might either of you ladies be seeking male companionship?"

"Excuse me?" replied Manuka.

"Let me introduce myself. My name is Mesquite."

"Buzz off, buster," Mustard said as she landed heavily on an adjacent blossom. "Neither are queens."

"Rats," Mesquite said, slouching immediately. "I never get lucky."

Mustard chuckled. "You males are all the same. After only one thing."

"Well, it's not like anyone thinks we're good for much else. At least you get to have stingers," he said.

"Hey, it's a serious responsibility," Mustard replied, waggling a finger. "Takes a lot of sand to keep the peace, as these two saw earlier."

"That's right," Manuka said, remembering. "Why didn't it kill you to use your stinger?"

"No barbs," she said, leaning over and showing them. "Mine's smooth. Yours isn't."

Manuka stole a glance behind at her own. Yes, definitely barbs.

"And I've got nothing," Mesquite said dejectedly.

"You've got your duty," Mustard offered with a grin.

Mesquite sat down on his blossom. "But what if I never find a queen? Most drones at our hive haven't. We just wander around, looking. We don't even get to be foragers. And if we do find a queen, we retire inside the hive and are never seen again. What's the point of it all?"

"Where is your hive?" Cotton asked.

"On the other side of the island, near the water. It's not very big, but we're still struggling to find flowers these days," he replied.

"I told our queen and the colony that we should let you guys help forage," Manuka said. "They thought I was nuts."

"But that's not a new thing," Cotton said, smiling.

"That was really brave," Mesquite said appreciatively. "No one in my hive would stand up for drones like that. We just get kicked out every morning and commanded to go find queens or die trying."

"Well, the blossom shortage isn't helping the bee or the queen population, that's for sure," Mustard added. "We were lucky to find this patch today at all. I've been thinking we need to cross the water to see what's there."

"Can bees really fly that far?" Cotton asked.

Mustard stood up and dusted off her ruff. "It takes a while to build the stamina for a flight like that, but my top foragers and I should be able to handle it."

"Do you need our help?" Manuka offered.

Mustard shook her head. "No. It's too dangerous for young bees like you. Better stay here."

"Do you think there might be queens over there too?" Mesquite asked hopefully.

"Only one way to find out, Romeo." Mustard grinned. "We go over at first light tomorrow, if you want to join us. We'll meet here." She turned to Manuka and Cotton. "Time to head home, girls."

Mustard led them through the crowded main hallway of the bumblebees' hive inside the rosebush. The floor and ceiling were made of smoothly padded dirt instead of wax, and there were side tunnels and alcoves filled with bunks. All the bees, young and old, regardless of class or job, seemed to be grouped haphazardly together. Many even shared acorns full of honey, passing them back and forth, chatting happily between slurps. Occasionally, Manuka and Cotton were noticed as newcomers, but the bumblebees would shrug their shoulders and resume their conversations, ignoring them.

Mustard selected a couple of bunks in a small alcove with five other bumblebees and then brought them another acorn of their own to share.

"After you finish this, you're expected to join us in the top branches of the rosebush. The queen will be there, and she usually tells us a bedtime story." She smiled extra broadly at Manuka.

"We'll be there," Manuka said, hoping this would be the promised chance to learn what was so special about her name.

"Can you believe the queen tells them a story *every* night?" Cotton asked in wonder.

"This hive is awesome," Manuka said.

Chapter 5

Just as Mustard said they would, the bumblebees gathered together in the twilight. The air was cool, and a soft breeze rustled the branches around them, while the sunset colored the sky a delicate peach.

After the bees quieted, the queen appeared and sat herself down comfortably on a branch with her back against the trunk. Her smile was as broad as her belly, and Manuka noted that she was larger and taller than even Mustard.

"Good evening, children. We are joined by some very special guests," she said, nodding to Manuka and Cotton, "so tonight, I will tell you an equally special story. Many of you have heard it before, but it's always worth telling again. This is "The Secret of Honey":

"Long ago, the world was covered in flowers of every size and hue. In fact, flowers were so numerous that bees barely flew at all but instead hopped from blossom to blossom, drinking sweet nectar that seemed to be in endless supply.

"Back then, bees didn't need to work all day making honey and storing pollen. Instead, they lounged contentedly on petals in the sunshine, watching the clouds drift by.

In the evenings, they returned to their hives to sleep, and their broods were numerous and ever growing.

"But then, one day, the sky darkened, and a heavy, dust-filled cloud blotted out the rays of the sun. The bees assumed the sun would return, as it always had, but it didn't. After a few weeks, most of the flowers began to dry up, and soon the bees were starving, but not being able to adjust, they went back to the dying flowers every day to try to find nectar that wasn't there. At night, weak and hungry, they returned to their hives and cried bitter tears of despair in their beds.

"But there was one little bee who couldn't abide watching her siblings' suffering any longer; so she decided to try something new.

"Nearby there was an ancient and powerful Manuka Tree that served as the spirit of the Great Flower Meadow where the bees lived. She sat quietly by herself, day in and day out, waiting for the time she would be needed. One morning, the little bee went to her, knelt, and begged forgiveness on behalf of all the bees for their great hubris in taking the sun and flowers for granted.

"She prayed to the tree through the day and all night, braving predators that had grown bold, for the nourishing rays of the sun to return and waited for the wrinkled face she thought she could see in the tree's trunk to answer.

"Finally, morning came, as dusky as ever, and she woke and saw that the tree had bloomed a million white flowers on its branches and had wept golden tears that were pooled at the bottom of its trunk. Drawn by the fragrant smell, she stepped forward cautiously and tasted the tears. They were sweet, like nectar, but much more nourishing, and her stomach immediately stopped growling.

"She gathered a cupful of the liquid in her hands and raised it high above her head. 'Thank you, Manuka Tree,' she said. 'We will never take anything for granted again.'

"At that moment, the clouds parted, and a single ray of the sun darted through, lighting the nectar she held aloft with a golden fire that radiated outward in a thousand spokes. As the solution grew hot in her hands, she brought it down and saw that it had become more concentrated and now glowed of its own accord as the rays of the sun had now become captured within it.

"'You have been given a gift,' said the tree. 'What you hold is pure energy itself. It will sustain you and your kind for generations to come. Learn to make it, store it, and protect it, and you will never go hungry again.'

"'We are grateful, and we will never forget.'

"'That's true, because today, I give you a new name, which is the same as my own. You shall be known as Manuka. You will be queen of your hive, and you will build your colony here in my branches so you will always be close to my flowers which, I promise, will bloom whenever you need them.'

"Manuka did as the tree said and led the bees to a new place in its branches. Her hive became the largest and strongest that ever was — so large that new colonies were spawned from it and took residence in the surrounding meadow.

"Eventually, the sun returned, and the flowers bloomed everywhere again, but this time, the bees were hardier due to the tree's magical nectar. Also, they had learned the value of hard work and how to make their own honey from the nectar of its flowers.

"Manuka grew very old and stayed with the tree, sitting in its branches and marveling at the prosperity of the bees. In the early evenings, when the work was done and the bees were rested after their last meal, they would visit her, gathering around in a circle, and she would tell the story of how the Manuka Tree saved them and taught them the secret of honey.

"As the years went by, bees of every type spread everywhere. They worked and thrived and worked some more, but they never forgot Manuka or the tree's promise — and they never took the sun or the flowers for granted again."

The queen smiled and let her story's close linger over the hushed crowd for a few more seconds. Then she stood, opening her thick arms widely. "May we all appreciate and give thanks for our gifts, just like Manuka. It has been another long day, and I'm sure you're all very tired. I bid you good night and wish you a restful evening."

The bees yawned and stretched as they stood, softly murmuring to one another as they flew out of the branches and began to descend to the earth. Manuka knew she should be tired as well, but she couldn't quiet her mind, which seemed to be humming along on the power of the queen's story.

"I always thought your name was for some flower. I never would have thought it was associated with a story like this," Cotton whispered.

Mustard approached them. "I said you would find out about your name later. Would you both like to meet Queen Prickly Rose?"

"Are you sure her attendants would be okay with it?" Cotton asked.

"What attendants?" Mustard said, clearly puzzled. Then she shook her head in frustration. "I told you. We're not like the honeybees. Everyone talks to everyone here. I speak to the queen every day myself. Come meet her. You'll be glad you did."

Manuka and Cotton followed Mustard's swaying girth toward the queen, who was chatting amiably with a couple of other bees. They waited until her conversation concluded and then approached her.

"So these are our two famous interlopers," the queen said with a grin. "I'm told you have been helping our hive with our foraging. You are most welcome here, whatever the cause for your visit."

"Thank you, Queen Prickly Rose," Manuka said, bowing. "We loved your story as well."

"Yes, I'm sure you did," the queen said. Her light brown eyes sparkled knowingly. "Your queen must truly think highly of you to give you such a legendary name."

"Your Majesty, I don't know exactly why she named me Manuka. Actually, we've never heard the secret of honey before. We don't really tell stories in our hive."

"No storytelling?" The queen's brow furrowed. "That is surprising. Still, your queen must know the story herself somehow."

Manuka nodded. "She must. Maybe if we ever get back, I can find a way to ask her."

"Mustard said your hive is struggling to find enough flowers too, and something is wrong with your honey."

"Yes, our queen told the hive that we wouldn't have enough honey to last the fall and winter. As to the honey being poisoned, that's what Cotton and I believe. Many of the bees are sick and dying. Even the queen is sick. We tried to tell her, but that's why we were kicked out."

The queen's pity was plain on her face. "Well, we're glad to have you. Our hive is small and very simple, but you'll find warmth and friends here. You're welcome to stay as long as you want, and there is no space inside forbidden to you, including my quarters. Now, if you'll excuse me, I must retire."

They said their goodbyes and watched the queen leave. Mustard turned to them. "Like I said, not like the honeybees."

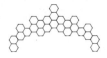

Manuka's thoughts were still churning as she tried to settle down in bed.

What could have been Queen Trillium's reason for naming her Manuka? Was she planning to tell her at some point or was it up to Manuka to find out for herself?

Manuka had always felt out of place in her hive. Was her name the cause of her uniqueness, as if a magical destiny had been evoked with it, or had she simply been born odd? What did Trillium know that she didn't?

Flipping from one side to the other did nothing to lessen her agitation. After an hour or so, she gave up, leaned over the side of her bunk, and whispered down to Cotton, "You awake?"

"Who can sleep with you mangling the covers up there?" Cotton replied irritably.

"I was just thinking about destiny," Manuka replied.

"Of course you were."

"I was just thinking that we all have to have a purpose, don't you think?"

"Yes, if our purpose is to sleep and somehow find a way out of this mess and get back to our hive…"

"I'm not talking about that," Manuka interrupted. "I'm talking about a real purpose. Something we're supposed to do with our lives."

"The queen's story really got you riled up, huh?" Cotton said, flipping over.

"Yes. And I'm thinking I've got this name for a reason. Maybe I'm supposed to find the Manuka Tree again."

Cotton gave an audible sigh. "Manuka, that's just a story to help bees realize they shouldn't take anything for granted."

"You don't think it really happened? I do."

"Well, you would, wouldn't you? Can we please just go to sleep?"

"We all have a purpose, Cotton, and now I know what mine is. Tomorrow, I'm going over the water with Mustard. I'm going to find the Manuka Tree, and I'm going to bring back the nectar to heal the queen and our hive. You want to go back? That's the only way."

"So you say," Cotton said angrily, pulling the covers over her head. It was the last response Manuka would get out of her for the rest of the night.

Chapter 6

Manuka opened her eyes slowly and recognized the dirt ceiling of the bumblebees' hive. The remnants of her dream flickered in her consciousness, and she grasped at them before they seeped from her memory. She had been fleeing a vicious swarm of wasps, dodging and diving through another dense thicket. Then, just as she emerged from a bush and into the clearing, the tree was before her. Its immense branches were filled with white flowers, and the sun's rays shone behind it, gilding the edges of its leaves as they rustled in the wind. She rushed toward it as fast as her wings could carry her. The wasps ragged screams and whirring wings came louder as they too increased their speed and began to close the gap.

The tree seemed to beckon her forward with outstretched branches, but still she didn't know what would happen once she reached its interior. Would she be safe or would she be killed anyway?

She woke before learning the outcome.

She rose to sitting and rubbed her striped temples. After a minute or two, she hopped down to get Cotton's opinion.

But Cotton wasn't in her bunk.

"Do you know where my friend is?" she asked the two bumblebees who were groggily getting out of bed in the opposite bunks.

"No idea," said one, scratching the ruff of fur at the back of her neck. "Maybe she went to the Common Ward to get some food?"

Manuka made ready to go find her, but something in Cotton's bunk caught her eye. It was a thin piece of resin with writing on it. She picked it up and read:

Dear Manuka, I know you won't understand this because you never listen to me anyway. I've decided to try to return to our sisters. We don't belong with the bumblebees. We don't belong anywhere if it's not with our own hive. I'm tired of you constantly getting us into trouble and never listening to anything anyone else has to say. So far, you've succeeded in getting us banished. What's next?

Whatever it is, I won't have any say in it because it's clear you'll continue to blunder along, now claiming that it's your destiny to do so. Well, I may not know what my destiny is, but it's not to die for no reason. If I succeed in getting Acacia to forgive me, maybe I can do the same for you. If I do, I'll send word to the bumblebees that you can come home. If not, I wish you the greatest luck in all your adventures. Cotton.

Manuka felt tears well in her eyes, and her hands shook slightly as she held the resin. What did Cotton mean about Manuka never listening to her? She felt she was listening all the time to Cotton's constant scolding, her endless warnings. And what was wrong with believing in her own destiny? Just because Cotton didn't believe wasn't a reason for Manuka not to. And was she implying that

Manuka would get her killed? It was crazy. Manuka had done everything she could to protect her.

Manuka angrily tossed the resin in Cotton's bunk and stalked out into the main hallway, hoping to find Mustard. To her disappointment, she learned from a guard that Mustard had already left with a group of foragers to fly over the water. This made her feel all the more aggravated, so she wandered outside to get some air and try to figure out what to do next.

She found a fallen branch and took a seat. How could Cotton just leave without telling her? They were friends, weren't they? She wondered further why she thought she would have *any* chance in persuading Acacia to take her back. That bee would likely kill her on sight.

Manuka stood, realizing her next move. She had to pursue Cotton and try to convince her to come back. If she didn't succeed, Cotton would surely be dead before the day was done.

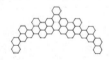

After fueling her flight with a few quick sips of honey, Manuka took to the air, flying through the thicket's brush in the direction of their hive. Once she emerged from its branches, she rose and continued in what she hoped was the right path. The world looked so different now in the sunshine versus the morning light that had illuminated their escape to Bombas Grove.

After a few minutes of flying, she heard a screech just above her and dodged in the nick of time as a pair of talons snapped shut where she had been. Another shrill chirp sounded, and she caught a glimpse of tan and brown feathers hovering just above her. She dove in alarm and flew into the boughs of an oak tree below. The bird screeched again and gained ground on her, its beak snapping ferociously. She spotted a small hole in the trunk and dove in, hoping the bird wouldn't be able to fit.

Once inside the darkness, she pressed up against the wood of the tree, feeling the dampness chill her wings and the fuzz on the back of her neck, and prayed to its spirit to protect her. After what seemed an eternity, she heard a series of chirps rattling outside. Ever so quietly, she crept to the rim and saw that the bird was fighting with another with an orange chest. Nearby was a small nest containing a pair of blue eggs. It was clear the new bird was guarding them due to the ferocity of her attacks. Finally, the tan and brown bird flew away, squawking indignantly, and Manuka watched as the other bird strutted back to its nest.

She waited a while, considering what to do next. Clearly the world was much more dangerous than she ever anticipated. If she was going to find Cotton, she'd need help. Maybe if she got out of the tree, she could see if she could persuade some of the bumblebees at Bombas Grove to help her pursuit. Slowly, she crawled out of the hole and made her way to the back of the trunk, facing away from the bird with the orange chest, and flew as quietly as she could back in the direction she had come.

By the time Manuka returned, most of the bumblebees had departed for foraging or other chores. She noticed a small troupe standing near the entrance and approached them.

"I need help," she said. "My friend has run away, and I'm afraid she'll be killed if she returns to our old hive."

"Hey, it's the Manuka Tree bee," said one of the bees with a laugh.

"Yeah, you and your friend came yesterday, right? She ran off already?" asked another.

"Please, I need help," Manuka said. "I tried to get her back myself, but a bird nearly ate me. Can you help me find her? It's not that far."

"Sorry, but Mustard sent word we were to join her at the clover patch and make ready to cross the water," the first bee replied. "She wants a bigger group going over than she originally planned, for protection."

Manuka was crushed. None of these bees knew what was at stake. The only one who would understand was Mustard, and she was already gone.

That gave her an idea. "I'll come with you," she said. "Maybe I can convince her to send some of you with me or join me herself."

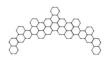

Manuka found Mustard with a group of ten bumblebees on the edge of the clover.

Mustard waved as they approached but stopped when she spotted Manuka. "What are you doing here?" she said as Manuka landed.

"Cotton is gone," Manuka answered, her voice wavering. "She left this morning while I was asleep."

"Are you really that surprised?" Mustard asked.

"Yes, of course I am!" Manuka replied. "She's my best friend. I never would have left *her*."

Mustard cocked an eyebrow and shrugged. "It's her life, Manuka. Sounds to me like she decided to live it instead of following you into whatever jackpot you land in next."

"Won't you come with me to stop her? There might still be time."

Mustard shook her head. "Sorry. I have duties to my hive, and the first of those is to find food. We're going over in a few minutes. I suggest you spend the day here and then return with the remaining foragers to Bombas Grove."

"But…" Manuka began, but Mustard had already turned away and walked to the front of the group, waving her hands in the air to get everyone's attention. Manuka saw Mesquite sheepishly glance at her from the far edge of the group. It seemed he was still determined to try to find his queen.

"Listen up! We fly over in standard swarm formation. I'll be at the front, leading the way. Flax will bring up the rear." She nodded toward the first bee Manuka had spoken to back at Bombas Grove. "Keep in mind that predators may assault us from above. If that happens, I want Hyacinth and Lily in the top center of the swarm with stingers ready. Mesquite, you stay near the bottom. Everyone, keep in mind if you land in the water below us, you'll likely drown or be eaten by a fish. Hence, we'll stay relatively high. Fly as fast as you can to keep up, and hopefully, we'll all get through this alive."

Manuka watched the bees fan their translucent wings as they made ready for the trip. She didn't know what to do, and the feeling struck her as bizarre. Was she supposed to go after Cotton again alone or should she stay in Bombas Grove? Life at Bombas Grove was empty if Cotton wasn't there. She saw Mustard give the signal and, all at once, the bees took flight. As they filled the air, the decision took shape inside of her: She would go with them. Cotton had chosen her path, now she would choose hers. Hopefully her destiny and the tree was at the end of it.

To keep up, she would need energy. Frantically, she searched the flowers for a vacant bud. Seeing none, she noticed an insect with huge, flat, multicolored wings sipping daintily on the same luscious yellow daisy she had visited the day before. She flew over and knocked it, spluttering, onto the ground. "What the... How *dare* you!" she heard it yell from below. She mashed her face into the flower and sucked in several giant mouthfuls of nectar. A surge of energy immediately followed. She leapt into the air in pursuit of the bees, who were now a third of the way across the water, and flew as fast as she could.

She surprised herself when she caught up quickly, flying a few feet above the swarm. Mustard felt her shadow and looked up. "Manuka! What are you doing?"

"I'm coming with you!" she shouted back.

"You fool girl! You're out of formation!"

"So make room for me!" Manuka replied. She was about to descend when something huge and gray hurtled just in front of her, scattering everyone. It rose again, and she watched it snap its yellow beak at the bees, who were attempting to sting its white head while it squawked. Then another fell out of the sky, followed by another, and another. Manuka got knocked sideways by the tip of one bird's wing and rolled over. They were everywhere, and she dove to escape. Below her, Mustard was bellowing to the few bees that were still together. "Run! Fly as fast as you can to the other side!"

"Shouldn't we go back the way we came?" Manuka shouted.

"That's where they came from!" Mustard replied.

As another bird lunged for Manuka, she dove straight down toward the water to avoid it but pulled up just before she hit the deep blue undulating waves. Mustard came up behind her, screaming, "Get away from the water! You won't be able to fly if you get wet!"

"Where am I supposed to go?" Manuka screamed back.

"Follow me!" Mustard shouted.

Manuka did so, and together they flew a few feet above the waves. Out of the corner of her eye, she saw Mesquite was also flying with them. She hoped the reason the birds weren't pursuing them was because they were being overwhelmed by the bumblebees' defenses and not because they were enjoying a meal.

Chapter 7

After what seemed an eternity, they finally landed on a cluster of reeds that were poking out along the bank on the other side of the water. Manuka was breathing so hard she feared she might pass out. Mesquite didn't look much better.

"I don't know if it's any safer here than out there," Mustard said from the reed she was grasping in front of them.

"Do you think the others made it?" Manuka asked.

Mustard shook her head sadly. "I don't think so. I saw Flax and a few others hit the water. No way they're flying after that. The rest probably fled back the way we came. Or, at least, I hope they did."

"I'm sorry, Mustard," Mesquite said.

"Thanks," Mustard replied. "Now, we need to find some cover."

Mesquite nodded and pointed at a large dark brown structure looming farther up on land. "What about that?" It had straight sides and a pointed roof. Also, there were dark squares cut out of the side facing them that made Manuka feel as if it were watching and listening.

"Are you sure it's safe?" she asked.

"Safer than sitting out here in the wind waiting to be picked off by more birds," Mustard replied.

"What do you think?" Manuka asked Mesquite.

"Anything is better than getting eaten," he replied.

"Exactly," Mustard said.

Mustard flew toward it, and they followed. There was a crack in a sheet of what seemed to be a clear resin covering one of the square openings of the structure. One by one, they each crawled inside as quietly as they could. The interior was dim, musty, and fairly empty. They landed on the wooden floor in a spot that was bathed in sunlight from a square opening above that was covered by more clear resin.

"What is this place for?" Mesquite asked, staring up in awe at the ceiling that soared above them. His black antennae stretched out curiously.

"It was a place where the Great Builders made things," said a velvety voice that floated down from a high ledge. They turned and saw a brown, eight-legged body with black stripes emerge and carefully pick its way down the wall to them.

"Stop, Spider! We are armed!" shouted Mustard.

"Yes, I know, bumblebee. I am too, in case you didn't know," the voice replied in irritation. "I've already fed anyway, so you have nothing to fear." She made it to the floor and took a few steps toward them. "Besides, why would I attack a group of bees when there are fluttering moths to snatch every night at my window?"

"What do you want?" Mesquite asked.

"To talk, of course. I so rarely meet anything worth talking to, and bees always seem to have news."

"Stop right there," Mustard said. "What do you want to know?"

"Oh, I don't know." The spider gently sat herself down, crossed her forearms in front her, and tilted her head playfully to the side. "What's new?"

The bees hesitated, looking at one another. Manuka was transfixed by the spider's face. She counted eight black eyes in all, and when the spider caught her looking, she winked one of them at her and smiled.

"What's your name?" Manuka asked.

"Goldenrod."

"Who are the Great Builders?"

The spider smiled again. "The Great Builders are those who made these structures. They're a lot like bees, actually. They build massive hives of their own, where every builder has their own space inside the larger structure. My cousin lives high up on the side of one not far from here. If you fly inland enough, you'll see a number of them."

"But why aren't they here now in this one?" Mesquite asked, crossing his arms.

"Because they enjoy discarding as much as building," Goldenrod replied. "Lucky for us spiders, we get to inherit the remains and live in a nice insulated hunting ground."

"They must be very big bees." Manuka said, looking up at the ceiling again.

"Oh, they're not bees. They don't have wings or stingers, fur or antennae. But they make up for it all in size. Plus, they seem to be absolutely terrified of us, which is always worth a giggle." Goldenrod chuckled. "Still, if you see one, I would stay well away. They'll likely try to smack you dead. Luckily, I'm quick."

"Isn't there one of those resin structures on our island?" Mesquite asked Mustard.

"Yes, on the far end. But Builders don't live in it. They keep plants inside. We tried to get in a few times, but they have it sealed up pretty good."

"So what brings you here?" Goldenrod asked.

"There's a drought, and we're having trouble finding enough flowers, so we're trying to find new foraging grounds," Manuka offered.

"That's very brave of you."

"We don't need compliments from an eight-legger," Mustard said. "And we don't have time to sit around and shoot the breeze, either."

"That's a shame, because I have something that will help you on your journey," Goldrenrod replied. "Oh well, I guess someone else will appreciate it instead." She turned as if to go.

"No wait!" Manuka said. "We want it."

"You do? How wonderful. Let me see, I have it right here somewhere. Oh darn, look at that, it's stuck to my spinneret. Pesky silk, always getting tangled up. Could you help me unravel it?" Goldenrod turned around to show her.

"Sure." Manuka took a few steps forward, her eyes cast down, looking at the spinneret.

Mustard and Mesquite saw Goldenrod's head turn to watch Manuka intently, her jaws opening slightly in a sneaky grin.

"No!" Mustard shouted and darted forward, just as Goldenrod jerked around and lunged.

Mustard grabbed Manuka by the waist and snatched her out of the way in the knick of time. She pulled her up high into the air out of reach and flew onto a wooden beam a few feet above. Mesquite joined them there.

Goldenrod chuckled as she looked up at the three of them and resumed her sitting position, as if nothing had happened. "Well, you can't blame me for trying."

"Want to bet?" Mustard shouted down to her. "You all right?" she said to Manuka, who she was still holding.

"Yeah, fine." Manuka felt a little dizzy and wondered how Mustard had guessed the spider was about to lunge.

"Well, it wasn't personal," Goldenrod said in Manuka's direction. "Good luck on your travels. There's an exit over there," she added, pointing gracefully with one of her legs toward the far end of the structure. "And, if the carpenter bee I dined on last night was telling the truth, there's a few daisies outside to fuel your flight."

Manuka stifled a shudder but managed to be courteous. "Thank you."

"You are most welcome," she said, raising herself up and turning around to amble back toward the wall. Over her shoulder, she added, "I believe if you head north, you'll find even more flowers… and a bit more."

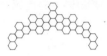

After they drank the nectar of the yellow daisies, the group spent the next few minutes grooming themselves to remove accumulated dust from their coats. Mustard joined Manuka on her blossom and began dusting off the back of her brown shoulders and between her wings.

"Manuka, we need to talk," she said. "If we're going to survive this forage, you need to start heeding me."

"I have been…"

"Let me finish. One of the reasons we might have been attacked so quickly when we went over the water was that you were out of formation."

"But I tried to come down to you…"

"Manuka, I know you have a hard time controlling your impulses, but now, more than ever, is not the time to give in to them. There are predators everywhere…"

Manuka let her drone on. Mustard was beginning to sound like Cotton. She felt a twinge of guilt but pushed it away. Then she remembered the queen's story about the tree. She could practically see it blooming right in front of her. She knew it was out there waiting for her somewhere. If only she could find it, she could bring back the nectar and heal her hive. Then Cotton would forgive her, Queen Trillium would be proud of her, and everything would be right again.

"Are you listening to me at *all*?" Mustard asked, giving her a pinch.

"Ow, yes! Just because you don't know what to do doesn't mean you should be pretending to lead others. My ideas are just as good as yours."

"Are you sure about that?" Mustard replied. "Have you ever foraged at all? You didn't even know about the Great Builders or that Goldenrod was dangerous. Everyone outside a hive does."

Manuka shrugged her off and turned around. "At least I know what it means to have a *real* purpose."

"What are you trying to say?"

"Just that we should be trying to find the tree, not another cluster of flowers. You can search for them, and I'll help you, but ultimately I'm after something else."

Mustard hesitated as she processed what Manuka said. "You believe you can find the tree? It's a legend."

"Are you sure Queen Prickly Rose would agree?"

"Of course I am. She wants us to find flowers so we can survive. She doesn't want us chasing fantasies."

"Well, I'm not part of your hive, am I? Guess I can do what I want."

"Not if you continue to act on your own and put us all at risk."

Manuka set her jaw. "Are you asking me to leave?"

Mustard hesitated. "No. But you better starting thinking a whole lot more before you act, or you might get us killed." She flew off before Manuka could launch a retort. As she watched her join Mesquite, Manuka licked away some crusted nectar from the side of her mouth. It had been sweet, but now there was a slight tinge of bitterness to it.

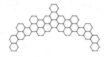

Laurel hopped into the Down Shaft because it was the fastest way to get to Acacia, who was waiting for her in the Restricted Ward. The guard who had come to get Laurel in her room said the matter was urgent, so Laurel threw on a robe and scuttled out as if her chambers were on fire. It didn't do these days to keep Acacia waiting.

In the Down Shaft, Laurel tried to keep her eyes focused on where she was heading and not on the single emaciated worker bee that fluttered precariously just below her. Because the honey was running out, rations were getting smaller and smaller, and those bees that weren't already sick or dying were suffering malnutrition. Laurel herself had a small store of pollen in her room, which had sustained her over the past few days. With a twinge of anxiety, she wondered what would happen when it ran out. Would Acacia grant her another share?

It was anyone's guess, really. Laurel had overheard two guards talking outside her room the day before about how Acacia had banished a forager for asking whether it made sense to swarm to a new place. Even though it had been their pre-agreed objective, Laurel wondered if Acacia would do the same to her if she brought it up now. Maybe banishment would be better than what lay ahead.

She arrived at the level of the Restricted Ward and got off, thankful at least that she didn't have to look at the skinny bee anymore. She walked to the entrance, gave her name, and entered.

A year earlier, this area had been part of the Drone Ward but, since it was rarely used, Acacia had appropriated it for her own "special projects" as she described them. Given her success in teaching the drones to fashion spears, Queen Trillium approved the reallocation of the space, and Acacia had spent a considerable amount of time here ever since. Laurel had never been allowed in before.

On her way down the corridor, she passed two chest-high capped pods filled with the chemicals they used to poison the hive's honey. Two bees had died bringing in the foul liquid, and ultimately, only an acorn capful had been needed to poison the hive's entire supply. Looking back now in shame, she couldn't believe she had been so foolish to think that just a tiny bit wouldn't have disastrous results.

Up ahead, she heard a puzzling series of hoarse screeches. Was there a strange bird caught in the hive? She picked up the pace and reached the main area of the ward but halted in shock.

Acacia, who was standing in the center of the room wearing a gown made of lustrous blue morning glory petals and talking to Coriander, noticed her and walked over, smiling. "Amazing, aren't they?"

Laurel's face was ashen as she stared at fifty cages, each housing a full-grown wasp. "I don't understand. What…"

"You don't like a few extra houseguests?" Acacia laughed, in a rare instance of mirth. "Well, I suggest you get used to them as there's more coming."

"Why?" Laurel said. "I mean, why wasps?"

"Because no one *else* has them," Acacia said. Her eyes were flat again, without a trace of humor. "We'll be able to claim any territory we choose, near or far. Hence no need to swarm."

"Yes, but there are other insects besides bees," interrupted Laurel.

"You think any of them will stand their ground against a horde of wasps?"

"A horde?"

"Come with me." Acacia turned and walked toward another passageway leading out of the room. Laurel followed. A feeling of incredible dread was getting cozy with her usual feeling of helplessness. They arrived in a smaller room that was filled with a cage double the size of the others. Inside, a giant wasp sat quietly, watching them with yellow eyes. Her heavy breath was the only noise in the room. Laurel was speechless.

"A queen," Acacia said proudly. Her black antennae twitched happily in her thatch of jet-black hair. "She'll raise hundreds more for us in a New Order that will make ours the most powerful hive that ever existed."

"You're insane," Laurel whispered.

Acacia stayed eerily silent for a beat. "You just wish you thought of it first. You'll always be a secondary player,

Laurel, and the fact that you can't see the genius in this only proves it."

"I get it, Your Grace," said Coriander, as she joined them, standing just behind.

Acacia turned, glaring at her. "She's hungry," meaning the wasp queen. After Coriander slinked away, Acacia turned back to Laurel. "They need more nutrients than just nectar."

Coriander returned, carrying the body of a small dead bee. "Will this do?" she asked.

Acacia nodded and led Laurel away.

Instinctively, Laurel knew she needed to choose her next words *very* carefully or Acacia might decide the wasp queen's next meal would be a second attendant. "How are you going to explain this to Queen Trillium when she recovers?"

Acacia smiled slightly, as if to herself. "I'm confident it won't be an issue. Once the queen learns we'll never have to leave her precious ancestral home for any reason, she'll agree. In fact, that's why I summoned you here. I understand you've been keeping to yourself. From now on, I want you at the queen's side night and day, monitoring her care and anything she says. If she improves, notify me immediately. Do not tell her anything. Do not do anything else. Is that understood?"

Laurel knew she didn't have much choice either way. "Yes," she agreed.

"Good. Now, it's feeding time for the rest of the wasps. Assuming you don't want to lose your last meal, I suggest you go to the queen now." And then to a nearby guard she said, "Escort her to the queen's chambers. She's needed there immediately."

Laurel walked away as quickly as decorum would allow, wondering how things could get any worse.

Chapter 8

As they flew farther northward, Manuka saw many more hives of the Great Builders. Some were small and squat, others were tall and shiny and reflected in the sun as if they were made of water. Because she was getting used to flying high, looking down didn't upset her stomach as it had before. She noticed more grayish paths with moving boxes plodding along below and then, on other smaller paths, she saw what she thought were the Great Builders themselves.

"Is that them?" she said, flying in close to Mustard.

Mustard flicked her eyes down briefly and nodded.

"Can we go see them?" Manuka asked.

"Absolutely not!" Mustard said. "I don't give a fig for most of what that spider said, but even she was right about one thing: The Builders are fierce. They will flatten you if you go anywhere near them. Besides, this isn't a safari, it's a forage, and we have one task: find flowers. Now keep looking."

Manuka rolled her eyes. *Some of us are looking for more than just flowers*, she thought. She resumed her place in formation next to Mesquite.

"I don't blame you," he said. "I would love to see one of them up close."

"They sure look ugly from here. Notice how they're all one color and they don't have any wings?"

Mesquite nodded. "Look at all the stuff they made. It's everywhere. I never knew, living on the island."

"Me too. Do you think…" She stopped cold as a familiar heady scent reached her nostrils.

Mustard caught it as well and nodded. "Flowers are close. We should be on them soon enough."

In minutes, a huge meadow came into view. It was situated between two of the Builders' massive shiny boxes and seemed to have paths crisscrossing it. Already, they could see it was speckled with color. The hundreds of different aromas it exuded rose in a powerful wave, making their mouths water with renewed hunger.

"Hold up, you two! Don't go flying in all at once. Gather over on that pine tree for a minute," Mustard commanded.

They complied reluctantly and then, after landing, continued to gape at the sight before them. Wildflowers of every shape, size, and hue covered the field. Manuka couldn't begin to count them all or, in some cases, tell them apart, as their variety became a wash of color before her eyes.

"Amazing," Mesquite said.

"Yeah," Mustard agreed. "Something funny about it, though. Why is it so quiet?"

"We found the Great Meadow of the Manuka Tree, and you're questioning it?" Manuka asked. "It's a gift. What are we waiting for?"

"Just hold up a second. Let's come up with a plan."

"A plan for what? I'm going. Anyone who wants to come can." She flew off toward the meadow, ignoring Mustard's shouts behind her, and chose a beautiful orange milkweed as her first stop. To her right and left were purple hyacinths, red wood lilies, and blue irises. She considered that it *was* rather quiet for such a plentiful field but then thought that perhaps the other insects were more spread out due to the volume of flowers.

Mesquite flew in, landing on the neighboring iris. "Mustard suggested we buddy up for safety. Hope you don't mind."

Manuka nearly snorted the heady nectar she was already sipping from the milkweed through her nose. "Are you sure *you* don't mind? I seem to wear out my buddies."

"Aw, you're okay," Mesquite said. "A little opinionated, maybe, but not enough bees question authority anyway. Too bad you weren't born a queen; it would suit you," he added, casting his eyes downward.

Manuka laughed again. "Instead, I was born a troublemaker. Well, at least *you* can marry royalty."

"If I can find it," Mesquite replied with a grin. "It's unlikely, to say the least." He took a drink of the iris's nectar. "It *is* quiet here. I wonder where everybody is?"

"I think it's magical," Manuka said, lying down. Her belly was already getting full. The flowers waved on either side of the cornflower blue sky above her that was spotted with clouds. "With a place like this, the tree has to be nearby."

"You want to try to find the tree?"

"Why else was I named Manuka?

Mesquite was about to respond when they both heard a chattering come from directly below. "What is that?" he asked, sitting up in alarm and peering down. "You think it's dangerous?"

"If it were dangerous, we would probably know by now," Manuka said, looking over the side of the milkweed. "Let's go check it out."

"Wait, shouldn't we…" Before he could finish, Manuka hopped down into the darkness below. Mesquite groaned and then followed her. "Manuka, come back. I don't think we should be doing this by ourselves." It was dim and damp under the flowers. The bright spears of light that penetrated through the petals and leaves above illuminated the stalks of the flowers, the dirt, and a few dead leaves, but not much else.

Carefully, he walked further in, whispering Manuka's name as loud as he dared. Then, the same chitter came again, this time much louder than before. He ran towards it, hoping he wouldn't find Manuka in the claws of a predator.

Instead he found her kneeling before a small bird lying on its side, not a great deal bigger than a butterfly. It had a grey underbelly and bright, leaf-green feathers covering its head and back that glittered when caught in one of the sun's infiltrating rays.

Manuka turned to him. "She's hurt, though I can't tell where."

"Stop! She could be really dangerous."

"Technically, so am I if I decided to sting her. Besides, look at how small she is. Her wings don't seem to work. Maybe if we looked underneath her…" Manuka walked around toward her back and started feeling around. Suddenly, the bird jolted and uttered another bout of rapid-fire cheeps. "I think there's something lodged in her back," Manuka said, taking a step back to see more clearly. "Yes, I see it. Maybe I can pull it out."

"Why don't we just go get Mustard? She's got to be worried about us." Mesquite offered in desperation, though he knew it was futile.

Manuka leaned in, grasped on to something behind the bird and pulled. A second later she was holding up a thin shard of brown-colored glass. "Huh. Wonder how that got in there?" She dropped it, perplexed at how this bird could have been stabbed with a piece of amber. She turned back to the bird and gave it a gentle nudge.

"That any better? Can you move your wings now?" She grabbed one of the bird's wings and moved it up and down, which didn't cause any more squawking. The bird slowly opened her dark eyes, blinking them, in what seemed confusion. Manuka came around and cautiously waited to see what the bird would do next.

"You-save-me," the bird uttered so fast that the words seemed to blend together. Manuka and Mesquite looked at one another, not sure if they had heard her right.

"You–save–me–thank–you."

"You're welcome," Manuka said. "Can you fly?"

"Can't–fly–no. Feel–weak–no–nectar–no–food."

Manuka looked at Mesquite, who immediately threw up his hands. "Don't look at me. We can't bring her any nectar, and we certainly can't lift her."

"Of course we can bring her nectar. There's nothing but that above us. All we have to do is take a mouthful and bring it down to her…"

"And put it in her *beak*?" Mesquite asked. "She'll eat us alive."

Manuka rolled her eyes in exasperation. "Look at her. You think she's a threat in this state?" The bird had closed its eyes again in exhaustion. "Wait here with her. I'll be right back." She leapt into the air and was soon out of sight in the rustling flowers above.

Infuriated, Mesquite crossed his arms, paced and muttered to himself, "Can't believe this… Crazy bee doesn't listen to anyone…" and so on and so forth as the minutes passed. "Where on earth has she got to?" he said to himself in frustration. Then a crack sounded behind him followed by a frantic shuffle of leaves somewhere in the growth. "Oh no," he said.

Manuka dropped down to the right of him with her eyes squinting under bulging cheeks that carried a giant mouthful of nectar. She walked over to the bird and began prying at its beak.

"We need to get out of here. I just heard something." Mesquite said as he tried grabbing one of her arms to pull her back. She threw him off and managed to get the bird's beak open. Mesquite crossed his arms again and watched as Manuka fed her. Immediately, the bird's eyes fluttered open wide. Manuka jumped back as it raised its head and got up. It stood and took them in from different angles, twitching its head rapidly from side to side. It fanned its wings out, as if to test them and, suddenly, they became a frantic flapping blur. It reminded Mesquite more of a bee's wings than a bird's.

"Nectar-good-very-good-feel-better!" it chattered at them. "Get-more-nectar-now-come-now-now!" It leapt off the ground in a whir of feathers and disappeared into the brilliance above.

"I think she said we should come with her." Manuka said.

"I didn't hear that," Mesquite said, making one last effort to keep them out of the bird's affairs.

Manuka laughed. "Yeah, right. Anyway, I'm going after her." She flew into the air before Mesquite could say another word.

Alone now, he wondered, for just a second, if he should follow her at all. However, another shuffling noise sounded too close for his comfort nearby, making him jump. He shook his head and took to the air. With or without the ridiculous bird, he would probably end up following her anywhere.

Manuka searched the surface of the flowers for the bird, but there was no sign of her. In their short time below, the sky above them had grown thick with saggy gray clouds. Hoping the bird would return, she took a seat on a purple coneflower. Soon Mesquite came scrabbling up and joined her.

"So, what happened to your friend?" he asked, in a way that sounded like he was only being polite.

"Not sure," she replied, scanning the horizon and twitching her black antennae back and forth. "I thought for sure she said she wanted us to come with her."

"Well, that's a bird's brain for you."

"How would you know?" she asked.

"I wouldn't," he admitted. "I just think it's best to stay away from them."

"So you would have let her die down there?" Manuka asked.

"I didn't say that. I just thought we should have… I just didn't want you to get hurt."

Manuka was tongue-tied. She was used to bees telling her what to do because it made their lives easier to stay out of trouble but not used to being protected for her own sake.

A drop of water hit one of the petals of the cone-flower with a thud and then slid down, pooling in the center where they were sitting. Both bees immediately jumped up, brushing the moisture off their legs and bot-toms. Then another drop of water crashed down, followed by another and another. Manuka got hit with one in the head and gasped as the cool water ran down her back between her wings.

"We've got to get out of here," Mesquite said. "Should we fly or go back down?"

Mustard flew up. "There you are! I've been searching for you everywhere!" she hovered in the air before them. "We've got to find shelter fast before…" She got hit with a bunch of drops all at once as the rain started to pour down. She landed spluttering on an adjacent coneflower. Manuka, who was now completely drenched, was about to hop over and help her, but suddenly, a blinding white light and a deafening crack, as if a tree had been split in two, drowned everything out.

"We've got to get out of here," Mesquite said. "Quick, get down below."

"We can't," Mustard shouted back. "It'll be filled with insects by now, especially predators. They come up when it gets wet."

Another boom erupted behind them. "Well, we can't stay here," Manuka shouted back.

Then, a whir of wings filled her vision, and a thrust of air knocked Manuka backwards. She landed with her head in a puddle but, when she looked up though the tangled wet hair that fell between her eyes, she saw the green bird hovering before them.

"You-come-with-me-now!" it rattled at them. "Grab-on-now-big-storm!"

"We can't fly," Manuka shouted. "Too wet."

"Fly-now!" replied the bird.

"What is she talking about?" Mesquite asked Manuka.

"I think she wants us to grab on to her somehow."

"You can try, but you'll have to stay away from her wings. They'll knock you senseless."

"But her feet won't." Manuka looked at Mustard, who was on her knees coughing, soaked through. Manuka turned back to the bird and motioned her down. "Extend your feet!"

The bird complied, and she grabbed her lower leg and hugged it closely above the talon. "You grab her foot," she said to Mesquite. He did so, and the bird gripped him gently. "Now get her," Manuka shouted to the bird, pointing in Mustard's direction.

The bird swiveled around in the air and approached. "I'm not being carried by a hummingbird," Mustard shouted defiantly. Another thunderclap erupted nearby, and she winced. Manuka could see she was grinding her teeth in aggravation. "Oh fine!" Mustard said and hopped forward. The bird caught her in midair and immediately darted up and toward the trees that ringed the meadow. The bees clung on to her feet for dear life and were nearly drowned in the deluge of rain that enveloped them as they rose higher and higher. Gusts of wind, whipped up by the storm, roared at them from between the trees, buffeting the bird and nearly knocking her over. Still, she managed to stay level and continued to climb in flight.

"Are you sure *this* is an improvement?" Mustard screamed from under the bird's talon.

Manuka would have fired back a response but suddenly had to hold on tight as the bird veered sharply to the right to avoid a tree trunk. A minute later they landed on a solid surface, which turned out to be a high branch in a silver birch. The bird hopped over to a little mossy cup nearby that was affixed to the bark of the branch. She stuck her beak in for a second and then spit out a stream of water that had accumulated inside. "You-stay-here-sit-here-now-sit," she said, waving them forward with a wing.

Manuka led the way, and the others followed reluctantly. Soon they were all crouched sorrily together in the bottom of the nest, where the rain continued to pelt them.

"Still don't think its an improvement," grumbled Mustard. She was drenched from head to toe; the short black hair on top of her head lay limp and tangled.

Then the bird stepped in, jostling them aside with its clammy, scaled feet and sat, covering the opening with its fanned wings. Only its head was left out in the rain. The bees were protected.

"Next time you can stay in the storm then," Manuka said, not able to help herself. She sat with her back against the wiry fibers of the nest and closed her eyes. It was getting warmer with the bird's body heat, and she was exhausted from all the adventure and stress of the day. She leaned back against the nest and closed her eyes. Soon she was fast asleep.

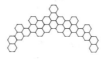

Manuka awoke in a tangle of bee bodies and bird feet. Something heavy was lying on her stomach, and she wondered if a stone had been dislodged from the nest somehow. When she looked down, she saw it was Mesquite's head. He was snoring softly. Gently, she moved him aside and on to Mustard, who was completely out. Manuka rose, parted the bird's feathers and poked her head out into the open air. The morning was still grey and fairly cool, but the clouds were a lighter color. Plus, they seemed to be higher in the sky than the day before. The bird opened her eyes, raised her head, and folded her wings. Manuka hopped out and faced her.

"You-better-now-all-dry-better?" the bird asked.

"Yes, thank you," Manuka replied. "You were so nice to save us like that."

"No-trouble-you-save-me-first!"

"Right," Manuka said, with a laugh. "I guess I did. What's your name, by the way?"

"Name's-Lilac."

"I'm sorry, could you say that again? Was that Slilac?"

"No-Lilac-Lilac-Lilac."

"Oh, okay. Lilac. I get it."

"How can you understand her at all?" Mustard said, as she climbed stiffly out of the nest.

"She just talks fast. All you have to do is listen."

"Never heard of a bird talking at all," Mustard said, clearly puzzled.

"Have you ever tried talking to one?"

"Of course not. Birds eat us. They don't talk to us."

Mesquite tumbled out and shook the dust out of his fur. "Maybe she makes sense to us because she's more bug than bird. She *is* a nectar-drinker. Plus, she buzzes and hovers like a bee."

"She's still dangerous," Mustard said.

"She's my friend," replied Manuka, irritably. "Besides, since she knows the area, maybe she could tell us where the tree is."

Mustard groaned. "Not that again. Manuka, I don't have time for babysitting. I suggest you stay here for the day. I'm going to look for more flowers. Mesquite, you're welcome to join me."

"But does the rain mean the drought is over? Do we still need to search for flowers?" Mesquite asked.

"One storm doesn't fix all our flower problems at home. We still need to find new foraging grounds, and I didn't come all this way to return empty-handed." Mustard flew off without another word, leaving Manuka wondering why no one ever took her seriously.

Mesquite turned back to her. "She kind of has a point..." he began.

Manuka spun around and leapt into the air, flying away as fast as she could.

"Manuka, wait! I'm sorry!"

She turned and saw that he was already following her, so she flew faster. "Leave me alone!" she shouted. She was through with bees telling her what to do. Mesquite stopped and flew back down to Lilac, who was sitting on the branch, her head cocked to the side in a puzzled expression.

Manuka went to a nearby sugar maple on the edge of the meadow. After she landed on one of its branches, she noticed a queer pink and yellow flower affixed to the side of its trunk. Curious, she went over and gave it a sniff.

"You bees keep doing that, and I'll never get any sleep," the flower said drowsily. It turned around to face her, waving a pair of frilly yellow antennae and rubbing large black eyes.

Chapter 9

Manuka had never known that insects could be so, well, pretty. This bug was covered head to foot in long, fluffy, pink-and-yellow fur. Her wings, which she fanned slowly, were easily three times her size. Her large, doe-shaped eyes were covered in heavy pink lashes, and atop her head were the yellow antennae Manuka had noticed earlier, which were slightly white at the ends.

"What are you, if you don't mind my asking?" Manuka said.

The insect smiled and tried to stifle a huge yawn. "A moth," she replied. "A rosy maple moth, to be specific. Now, if you don't mind, cicada season is coming, and I need to stock up on shut-eye now, or I'll never make it through a month of their ear-splitting droning." She turned lazily back to the trunk.

"Okay. But, wait," Manuka said, causing the moth to turn around wearily. "Do you know why there are so few insects around? I mean, with as many flowers in the meadow, we thought there would be more bees at least, but we seem to be the only ones."

"Who's 'we'?" replied the moth.

"My friends and I. There's only three of us. We're foraging to find new flowers."

"Well, in that case, I suggest you turn around and head straight back to your hive. There are bees here, but they're not the sort who take kindly to visitors. Hunger will be preferable to what they'll serve you."

"Okay," Manuka replied, wondering why this moth was still here if the local bees were so fierce. "By the way, what's your name?"

"Tupelo," the moth said as she groomed one of her antennae. "And yours?"

"Manuka."

"Really? That's interesting. Doesn't your kind have a legend concerning that name? Something about a tree, I remember."

"Yes, you've heard of it? I was named Manuka so that I would find the tree one day."

"Is that so? Your queen must have a lot of faith in you."

"She does," Manuka said, putting a hand on her hip and trying to look as confident as possible. "Do you happen to know where the tree is?"

Tupelo hesitated and cleaned her other antennae thoughtfully. "You'll find things of tremendous value require tremendous sacrifice."

Manuka nodded vigorously. "Oh, yes, I understand." Having already sacrificed her place in her hive in order to save it, she felt she had a good handle on what it meant to surrender something you cared about for something you wanted.

"What do you hope to gain by finding the tree?" Tupelo asked, becoming more curious about this intense honeybee.

"I'll use its nectar to heal our hive and the queen, who is sick. *Please*, tell me where it is, if you know."

Tupelo sat and crossed her arms in front of her as she weighed how to answer. "I believe there might be one inside one of the Great Builders' structures not far from here."

"That's fantastic!" Manuka exclaimed. "I can't wait to tell the others!" She stopped as a new pungent aroma hit her nose. "That's it, isn't it?" she said, turning in the direction from where it seemed to originate across the meadow. On the other side, she saw a large reddish-brown structure and heard a clanging sound that echoed across the flowers. She turned back to Tupelo. "That's where the tree is, right?"

Tupelo shook her head. "Wait a second, Manuka. Let me explain."

"I'm tired of everyone telling me to wait!" Manuka shouted. "The sooner we find the tree, the sooner everything can be fixed. There isn't a moment to lose!" She flew off the branch and headed for the brown structure before Tupelo could stop her.

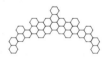

The musky perfume that emanated from inside the Builders' structure grew stronger as she approached it. She could see that it was larger than any of the other hives they had seen on their flight to the meadow and had countless clear resin holes, many of which were set in multicolored hues. Then, after circling the building, she came across the biggest flower she had ever seen.

It was set into the side of the structure, and its blossom had eight petals that were filled with mostly red and pink faceted pieces of resin, each the same diameter of a tree trunk.

"The Great Builders must worship the tree as well," she whispered in awe. "This must be one of its flowers." Below the massive blossom, an entryway stood open. She flew down to look inside and heard soft music and the hushed voices of the Builders who were all gathered inside together, standing in neat rows and facing forward. A cool waft of air from the interior caressed Manuka's face, carrying with it the strongest scent of the tree thus far.

"Manuka, wait! It's dangerous!" shouted Mesquite behind her as she began to enter. She turned, and he barreled into her, causing her to spin out of control into the interior. She landed harmlessly on a wooden plank and, once her eyes focused, saw two Builders standing right in front of her. An especially large one stood to the right and another one, much smaller, but still huge to Manuka's eyes, stood to the left. This smaller one had long hair that was folded ornately down her back and tied with a shiny lavender piece of twine. They were both singing softly, while looking down at flat objects they held before them.

"Manuka..." said a weak voice behind her, and she turned and saw Mesquite flopping helplessly in the corner of the wooden frame. She rose to go to him but, to her horror, saw that the smaller Builder, attracted by the futile buzzing of his wings, had turned and noticed him. She leaned down to get a closer look with huge blinking eyes that matched the color of the sky, and suddenly, she reached out with giant claws, enfolding him, and then raising him up as high as her waist. Manuka, alarmed, flew into the air, not sure if she should sting the Builder herself or go for help. Then Mustard appeared.

"How could you let her catch him?" she shouted at Manuka.

"I'm sorry! It happened so fast! I didn't know what to do!"

"Only thing to do now is sting her. I'm going in!" Mustard said.

"Wait!" Manuka said, pulling her back. "She might crush him."

"Or worse!" Mustard bellowed. "Builders tear the wings off flies. You think they treat bees any different?"

Manuka saw that the Builder was now headed outside. She didn't seem dangerous. Actually, she seemed to be treating Mesquite as gently as possible. "Just wait a minute, okay? Let's see what she does."

They followed her cautiously as she went out into the speckled sunshine with Mesquite still cupped in her hands. She approached a large red rosebush and placed him gingerly on one of the blooms, then turned around and went back to her hive.

Manuka and Mustard found him lying on his side in the center of the bloom, panting. "That was unexpected," he said with a weak smile.

"No kidding," Mustard said with a huff, glaring at Manuka. Tupelo joined them. "Who's this?" Mustard asked.

"That's Tupelo," Manuka offered.

"If you had waited, I would have been able to explain that the tree isn't inside that hive," Tupelo said wearily.

"How was I supposed to know?" Manuka felt her stomach curl up in embarrassment.

"Is she always like this?" Tupelo asked Mustard.

"Unfortunately, yes," Mustard grumbled and then turned to Mesquite. "Can you fly?"

He shook his head. "Don't think so. My wing hurts."

"You see what you did?" Mustard said to Manuka. "Now we've got an injured bee on our hands. All we need is a wasp or a hornet to come by."

"How about something worse?" said a large bee, who dropped onto the rose next to Mesquite. She was armored in white bark and brandished a long spear with a sharp amber tip. Immediately, twenty more identical bees carrying spears joined her, surrounding them.

They were ushered in a tight swarm by the armored bees back the way they had come. Several of those flying behind them kept spears pointed at their backs. Mesquite was arm-carried at the rear, his injured wing drooping painfully at his side.

In a whir of wings, Lilac suddenly appeared, blocking their path. "You-leave-friends-be-mean-bees," she shouted, parrying and thrusting her needle beak. The bees at the front immediately circled her, while Manuka and her friends were held back.

"Stupid bird didn't get the message last time. Finish her!" said the squad captain, who they had learned was named Foxglove. The bees moved in closer. A few distracted her while the others behind tried to assault her unprotected back.

"Leave her alone!" Manuka said, struggling to no avail against the guards that held her. "Stop it!"

Lilac turned in Manuka's direction, leaving her side unprotected, and Foxglove lunged, stabbing her in the soft tissue between her wing and breast. Lilac squawked and fell, disappearing into a clump of bushes just below them.

"No!" Manuka shouted, still struggling.

"Good," Foxglove said. "Let's move. The queen's waiting."

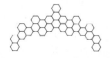

Their captors' hive was extremely large and sat in the sturdy top branches of an ancient and gnarled horse chestnut tree located on the northwest corner of the flower meadow. They entered through the hive's main entrance at the bottom and, once inside, were immediately thrust into the main passageway, which pulsed with marching bees, all carrying spears.

"To the Great Chamber," Foxglove said. They were pushed forward, shoulder to shoulder, into the rushing current of the tunnel.

"Killer bees. This is all we need," murmured Mustard, who was to Manuka's left.

"Is that what they are?" Manuka whispered back.

"The spears confirmed it. Only killer bees carry them."

"But…" Manuka was about to say that her own hive's guards carried spears too, but a guard smacked her roughly on the back of the head.

"No talking," she commanded.

As they continued, Manuka noticed that the so-called killer bees were almost completely black, except for the faintest of golden stripes that delicately covered the soft fuzz on their torsos. She felt the beginning of a notion start to form, but it was cut short when she bumped into Tupelo, who had stopped in front of her.

"Prepare to enter Queen Fireweed's chambers for questioning," Foxglove announced. The doors swung open, and they entered a large receiving hall. Similar to Queen Trillium's hive, it was oval-shaped, with a domed ceiling and high alcoves where workers fanned their wings, but also, in this hive, large chandeliers with glittering shards of twinkling amber and hundreds of lit wax candles cast a soft light on the group. The room was mostly empty except for the queen and her attendants, who were seated at the far end.

Manuka and her friends were brought forward and positioned in a single line, facing the queen, with one armored guard behind each of them. Tupelo stood to Manuka's right, while Mustard was at her left. "Whatever you do, don't tick her off," Tupelo whispered out of the corner of her mouth.

Queen Fireweed sat imperiously on her throne in front of them, blinking her large black eyes. Like the other killer bees, she was very dark, with just a few faint rings around her neck and torso. She wore a gown of yellow rose petals and an ornate crown of rare yellow amber that resembled frozen shards of creamed honey.

"These are the thieves our sentinels saw, Your Majesty," said Foxglove.

"What did we steal?" blurted Manuka.

"Our nectar, of course," responded the queen. "Everything in the Meadow belongs to us. You four found it and assumed you could take what you wanted. You were wrong. But what troubles me most is not what you stole. Any bee, or insect for that matter, within a mile knows to avoid the Meadow, but you didn't. Clearly, you're scouting for your own hives with a mind for taking the Meadow for yourselves. And someone was helping you," she added with a pointed look at Tupelo.

"Your Grace, they are just foraging bees, I assure you…" Tupelo began.

"That's rubbish," interrupted the queen. "There isn't a patch as large or as sweet as ours for miles and miles. I would know. I've sent my own scouts. You expect me to believe you weren't telling them our secrets so they could fly back to their hives and return with a horde to try to take it from us? That way you wouldn't have to forsake your precious maple trees, which you've been given one chance after another to leave. Well, time has run out on that as well."

Tupelo sighed and spread her hands in supplication. "Your Grace, I seek to live here in peace and harmony with your children. I have no interest in the flowers. My food is the sap of the trees where I nest. Nothing more."

"You can't own the flowers anyway," Manuka grumbled.

"Manuka, shut up," Mustard said through gritted teeth.

The queen froze and leaned forward. "What was that name?"

"Manuka," Mustard and Manuka said in unison.

"Blasphemy," the queen whispered, recoiling.

"What's blasphemy is finding a treasure as great as this and refusing to share it," Manuka said hotly. "Did you really chase away all the other insects? There's more than enough for us all. We're here because our hives are close to starving…" Her voice was cut off as a guard grabbed her from behind and shoved her to her knees. An amber spear was thrust under Manuka's throat so close that she could see her reflection in its honed blade.

"Shall I silence her once and for all, Your Majesty?" the guard asked.

"Hold off until we get to the bottom of this," the queen said, and Manuka was yanked to her feet.

"Your stupid spears don't scare me anyway. We have hundreds of them where I come from," she said.

The queen gave a dismissive wave. "That's nonsense. No one has the skill to make our amber spears."

"We do," Manuka crossed her arms. "Or at least one of us does. She taught our drones how to make them. You remind me a little of her, actually," she added as an afterthought.

Queen Fireweed's liquid black eyes narrowed. "What is this bee's name?"

"Acacia," Manuka replied.

Gasps erupted from the queen's attendants and guards, but the queen remained immobile, her hand gripping the armrest of her throne with her eyes fixed furiously on Manuka. After a second, she blinked and leaned back. "So the disgraced traitor survived," she whispered. Then, to Manuka, "I command you to tell me everything you know about this Acacia."

Manuka felt the whole room's attention focus on her, including the wide eyes of her companions. She turned back to the queen and responded, as truthfully as she could, "Only that she's a bully. Just like you."

Chapter 10

"You just couldn't keep your mouth shut, could you?" muttered Mustard as they were ushered by the guards into the killer bees' Confinement Ward.

"She asked me what I knew and I told her," Manuka replied.

"No, you told her off, more like it."

They arrived at a bank of cells all in a row and were each shoved into one of them. The bars were slammed shut.

"Wait, what about Mesquite?" Manuka asked in alarm, realizing he was the only one not in a cell and still being held by the guards. His face was especially drawn as he slumped in pain, still favoring his dragging wing.

Foxglove laughed. "Oh, we thought he could use some alone time. We've got a special solitary pod where he should be able to get some rest."

"Just hope we don't forget to feed him," another guard quipped.

"Or decide to fill the pod in with resin," replied Foxglove. She pushed Mesquite roughly in the direction they had come. He yelped and stumbled to the ground. "Come on, you worthless drone. Can't figure why we don't just toss you, but Queen Fireweed said you might encourage the others to be more helpful." She grinned at Manuka as they led him away.

"There. Are you satisfied now?" Mustard shouted at Manuka. "Whatever happens to him will be your fault!"

"How is it my fault?" Manuka said. "You're the leader. Not me."

"Yes, but you're the one who doesn't care enough about your friends to consider how what you do affects them."

"That's not true," Manuka said. Cotton came to mind. She had been a good friend to her. Hadn't she? She felt the sting of tears at the corners of her eyes.

"Oh, it isn't? I completely understand why Cotton left! She knew she was doomed if she stayed with you, just like we all are — even Lilac."

Manuka threw herself on her cot facedown, covered her ears, and curled her antennae in.

Mustard went to the bars of her cell. "You don't want to listen because it's true. At every single turn, you've done exactly as you pleased. And look where we are now. What do you think they're going to do to Mesquite? His wing is injured because you decided to run into that Builders' hive chasing your so-called destiny. Now they might hurt him even more just because you couldn't resist mouthing off to the queen."

"She *is* a bully," Manuka said into the blanket of her cot.

"So what if she is!" Mustard shouted. "I've had it with you, Manuka. You're not a friend to anyone but yourself, and, in my opinion, that makes you worse than any bully."

Manuka felt as if something sharp were being driven into her chest. She couldn't hold back the tears anymore and began to sob. She knew Mustard had to be wrong, but she couldn't find a way to argue with her. In her mind, images flashed of Cotton turning away, Lilac falling into the bushes, and Mesquite grimacing in pain. She had always wanted to help others, but it seemed that, right from the beginning, it always brought her trouble. Now she saw that the trouble she was bringing was not just on herself but on everyone she cared for. This made her cry even harder. Desperately, she hoped someone might try to soothe her, but only the silence met her tears, and she realized Mustard and Tupelo said nothing because they agreed. She carried on for some time, but after a while, exhaustion set in and, as the tears ebbed, sleep took their place.

Manuka could see the immense wooden door before her was slightly ajar. Soft golden light from the open crack spilled out onto the floor. High up in its center was the beautiful resin rose she had seen in the face of the Builder's hive. Its multicolored petals glittered from the warm light emanating behind it, and she knew once she passed through it, something amazing, something she had dreamed of time and again, but had never attained, would happen to her.

She ran forward, but suddenly, Acacia appeared, blocking her path. In her hands, she held a giant amber spear that caught the light from the crack in the door as she pointed it at Manuka.

Bewildered, Manuka tried to find a way around her but realized there was none because Acacia was already increasing in size, growing to almost half the height of the door. She smiled and thrust the spear's tip savagely at Manuka, who dodged it just in time but landed in a clumsy heap on the floor. She scrambled up quickly and saw that Acacia, who had now transformed into Queen Fireweed, was preparing to lunge again.

She jumped out of the way of the spear again and rolled away. Just behind Queen Fireweed, she could see the door was still open. She ached to go through it but saw the queen was raising the spear over her head, gripping it with both hands, preparing for another attack. She grinned, and Manuka watched in horror as she changed again, but this time, into Manuka herself.

"Who's the bully now?" her giant self said as she laughed, thrusting the spear forward.

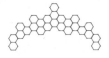

Manuka opened her eyes and saw she was still imprisoned, along with her friends. The others were already awake.

Mustard lay on her bunk quietly while Tupelo sat on hers, carefully cleaning her antennae.

She remembered the dream and wondered at its meaning. Was it possible that she had to conquer herself all along? Everything that had gone wrong had happened, in one way or another, because of her lack of self-control.

"What are you thinking about, Manuka?" Tupelo asked.

Manuka glanced at her and shrugged her shoulders. "I don't know. Just that maybe I owe you all an apology." She saw Mustard raise her black eyebrows in surprise.

"In fact, I know I do," Manuka continued. "You're right, Mustard. We probably wouldn't be here if I'd been more careful or listened to you. I'm so sorry. I'll try to do better."

Mustard remained silent.

"You clearly have a lot of passion," Tupelo offered. "You probably just need to control it better. Ultimately, it won't limit you; it'll take you farther than you dreamed."

That gave Manuka an idea. "What if I offer to tell Queen Fireweed about Acacia? Do you think she might let us all go?"

"It all depends on how you treat her." Tupelo smiled.

Manuka went to the bars and banged on them. Next, she tried to think of the smartest way to phrase her next words for the maximum effect. When the guard arrived, she said: "Tell the queen I have something she needs to know about Acacia right away." The guard ran off, and Manuka looked hopefully at Tupelo, who smiled. "That's a start," she said.

Chapter 11

From her forced-kneeling position, Manuka could just make out her own reflection in the floor's polished wax surface. The brown tufty fur on her head was sticking out in all directions and could have used some brushing. However, it would have to wait, as her hands were again tied uselessly in front of her with twine.

The queen exited her private chambers and approached the dais. She was wearing a simpler white gown of woven caterpillar silk and her crown. Manuka made as if to rise, but Foxglove, who was standing at her left, forced her back down. The urge to complain was overwhelming, but instead, she focused on her promise to her friends – that she would measure her words and deeds from now on. It wasn't going to be easy.

The queen sat down on her throne, and her attendants gathered around her. "You have something to tell me?"

Manuka took a deep breath. "Yes, Your Grace. I would be happy to answer any of your questions about Acacia. My hope is, if I do, you will free me and my friends and let us leave this place in peace."

"I see," the queen said. "What makes you think I won't simply have my guards force you to tell us what you know?" A light laughter followed from the group.

Manuka hesitated as she considered all the ways her former self would normally have countered and instead settled on a response she never would have chosen. "Because I've decided to believe that I was wrong earlier. Your Grace is not a bully."

The queen stayed silent, watching Manuka with interest. "She can stand," she said finally. The guards backed away, and Manuka carefully rose to her feet, unassisted. "Now, tell me," the queen continued. "What does this Acacia look like?"

"She appears to be completely black with no markings," Manuka began. "It's hard to tell because she always wears long robes. Also, she does resemble Your Grace in appearance, especially her eyes."

"All my daughters resemble me," the queen replied evenly. "But, yes, Acacia is all black. A rare trait. And, like me, she was born to be a queen."

Manuka was surprised at first but, after considering it, didn't know why. Acacia's imperious nature should have revealed her long before. "No one at our hive knows she's a queen," she said. "The story is she came to us long ago as a lost forager, seeking shelter. Our hive was in the midst of a wasp war at the time, and she offered to teach us how to make spears for defense."

"That's Acacia; resourceful as ever," the queen replied as she stood. "You'll join me now in my chambers so we can continue this conversation in private."

Manuka followed the queen to the interior of her rooms. Once inside, she was surprised to find the space fairly understated. Wax lanterns that hung from the ceiling provided soft, functional light. In the room's center was a sitting area, and situated here and there were a few small tables with vases of flowers that scented the room.

The queen chose a seat and gestured to Manuka to take a chair opposite hers. She gingerly removed her crown and placed it carefully on the table to her left, making sure it didn't upset the flowers or fall to the floor. Once that was done, she turned back to Manuka, looking less serious but visibly more weary. "Did she send you here?" she asked.

"No, not at all," Manuka replied. "She banished me and my friend, Cotton, from the hive when we tried to alert the queen of our suspicions that our honey is poisoned. If you ask me, I think she's the one who poisoned it."

"Are you sure the honey is poisoned?" the queen asked thoughtfully.

"No, we're not," Manuka admitted. "But if it's not, why are so many of the bees in our hive sick or dying? Even our mother, the queen, is sick." It dawned on her that maybe Acacia could be trying to take Trillium's place as queen, given that she was one herself, but she held her tongue.

"I see your thoughts in your eyes," the queen said. "But I hope you're wrong. True, Acacia can be ruthless;

I banished her myself for her outrageous behavior. Still, sometimes I wonder if her actions were partly my fault."

"You called her a traitor. May I ask why?"

The queen considered how to answer the question. "You said I remind you of Acacia. Well, you remind me of her. I reared Acacia to be a queen and replace me when I passed on, and I expected her to be headstrong, but I didn't expect her to be uncontrollable.

"In her early years, she explored nearly every part of the hive, even the Drone Ward, no matter how many times I ordered her to stay away from it. My attendants would catch her and send her back to her trainer for study, but she would always escape again. When she wasn't in training, she would harass her peers. The complaints I received on the disorder she was causing were endless. Obviously, I was cross with her, and she was punished frequently.

"It was a long time ago, but when I look back on it now, it seems her mind was always churning, either with new ideas or mischief. She seemed to want to be free of the structure of the hive and live as she pleased. Perhaps that's why sending her out on her own made so much sense."

"You sent her away?" Manuka asked.

"Not away, no. Just outside during the day. I assigned her a squad of guards, of course. Periodically, we had trouble with wasps as well, so I challenged her to see if she could find a remedy to the problem.

"Finally, after a week or so, she returned to the hive with something she had found at the base of a pine tree: a lump of golden rock so clear that you could see through it.

She asked me for permission to return to the Drone Ward to see if the males there could make something with it. Turns out they could. One drone, named Chestnut, who was apparently a very good shaper, found a way to chip off pieces of the stone, which we called amber, and fashion them into sharp points. These were made into spears using wood from our tree."

"I always wondered where the amber came from," Manuka murmured.

The queen seemed to have something in her eye that she brushed away impatiently. "Yes, well, I was very proud of her. It was the first time she had acted like a true queen, finding a solution to a problem instead of being the problem. I rewarded her with a larger squad of guards and more freedom to explore the world, which she did. Had I known what she would do, I never would have let her go." The queen stood and went over to one of the flower vases and began to arrange it very meticulously. Manuka wanted to ask a million questions but forced herself to wait patiently for the queen to continue.

"One day, a drone was killed in the Drone Ward. As you know, drones aren't born with stingers, so naturally, we went there to find the cause. What we found was unimaginable: ten full-grown wasps living in rudimentary cages in our own hive!" The queen slammed her fist on the little table in front of her, making the vase rattle on top of it. "At first, no one knew how they came to be there, but eventually, we got some of the drones to talk. They told us that

Acacia and Chestnut had been rearing them together. Both were brought in for questioning, and they admitted it.

"It turns out, on one of her forays, Acacia had been fascinated by a nearly empty wasp's nest that had been poisoned by the Builders and had decided to bring a small egg back with her to our hive. That egg grew into a wasp that laid more eggs. Acacia learned that if she kept the wasps' cages far apart, so they couldn't smell one another, and assigned them a single bee to care for them, they would imprint on that bee's smell and believe that one to be family. Each of the wasps we found was assigned to a member of her original squad, and that's not the worst of it; they were preparing to use them to take over this hive. Acacia and Chestnut were planning to be wed, and she would be queen in my place." At this, the queen crossed her arms in front of her body and bowed her head.

Manuka felt sorry for her. "You're sure of all this?" she asked.

"Well, how could I doubt it? Half of the story came from the drones, the other half from Acacia herself. I knew that I had been hard on her, but I never thought she would grow to hate me so."

"And you banished her?"

"She was given a choice: Builder banishment or death.

"What's Builder banishment?" Manuka asked.

"Instead of throwing a bee out of the hive, we take them to one of the Builder's shiny metal transports. When the builder opens the door, the bee is shoved inside and trapped. The Builder leaves and the bee is taken to another land, often too far away to ever find its way home. It's what we did to Chestnut and her guards, after we killed off her wasps. I begged Acacia to choose the same, but I wasn't sure if she would take it. In her extreme grief at losing Chestnut, it seemed she might prefer death. Fortunately, she decided to leave and my last gift to her was letting her leave on her own. Back then, I felt her treachery was unforgivable, but now I wonder if it still is."

Manuka wanted to be careful with her next words, but she knew the queen deserved the truth. "Acacia sent two wasps she was keeping in our hive after me and Cotton when she banished us."

The queen returned to her seat in front of Manuka. She looked more tired than ever. "It's all my fault," she said, half to herself.

"It can't be," Manuka replied.

"Perhaps if I hadn't been so angry and afraid, I would have handled it differently, and she would have learned from her mistake."

Manuka doubted that was true but kept her opinion to herself.

"I need to see her," the queen said. Someone has to talk some sense into her," She met Manuka's eyes. "Tell you what, you help me find her, and I'll let you and your friends go. We can start tomorrow."

Manuka wondered herself what would happen if they met up with Acacia but knew she didn't have much choice between that and freedom. "It's a deal," she said.

Chapter 12

The queen and about a hundred of her guards escorted Manuka and her friends in the direction of the island. Each of them carried an amber spear, and the queen had traded her crown for a breastplate of luminous white birch bark.

Mesquite was carried as before, given that his wing was still inoperable. Mustard had offered to house him at Bombas Grove until he was healed since his own hive might reject him due to his injury. Tupelo made an agreement with Queen Fireweed to join them and forsake her maple trees and find new ones in the territory that lay ahead. Manuka had tried to get her to share the location of the tree, but she remained reluctant, and Manuka couldn't determine why. She hoped, with more time, she could convince Tupelo to help her.

She wondered again what they might find when they returned to her hive. Would Queen Trillium be dead? If that were the case, the rest of her hive would likely already be gone without her scent to anchor them. But still, she couldn't imagine Acacia letting her live. The thought made her shudder.

They took frequent breaks as they flew, and after a few hours, they arrived back at the edge of the water. The queen chose a hollowed-out log for them to hide in near the shore. "We'll camp here tonight, so we're reenergized for the crossing in the morning," she said.

They found places inside and tried to get comfortable for the evening. Manuka and her friends huddled together as the sun set, watching it make the water outside the log glitter with orange sparkles. The depths below looked black, and Manuka wondered what could possibly live underneath.

Mesquite caught her hypnotized gaze and crawled a little closer. "I heard a forager once say she saw a giant silver fish as big as a squirrel leap out and catch a grasshopper in its mouth in mid-flight. It splashed back into the water and disappeared."

"Wow. If that's down there, can you imagine what else is?" Manuka asked.

"I know." Mesquite nodded. "I bet it's quiet, though. Maybe if we lived there, life would be simpler," he said and laughed.

Manuka thought about it and self-consciously brushed her hair out of her eyes, trying to smooth the tangles. "We would likely have other problems."

"That's probably true," he said. "But I bet we could do things our own way."

"Do you really wish that?"

"Of course." He smiled, brushing the dust off his arms and fuzzy brown and yellow-striped chest. "I wish I hadn't been born a stingerless drone with just one purpose. I have ideas of my own, you know."

"Like what?" Manuka was curious to hear just what shape a drone's ideas would take.

"Well, for instance, I'd like to make the drones foragers in addition to possible mates for queens. Most of us don't find queens, and it's not useful for us to spend all our time looking. Plus, it would give us a way to earn our keep in the hive so that we don't get kicked out come fall."

"That *is* unfair," Manuka said.

"Also, I believe drones shouldn't have to live in a separate ward. If we're all brothers and sisters to one queen mother, let's at least try to live together."

Manuka was impressed. "Have you ever said anything?"

"And be killed outright? Course not." He grimaced. "So, instead, I keep my ideas to myself. Except, of course, with someone like you," he added.

"Someone like me may not be who you want to confess your ideas to."

"Why not?" he asked, clearly perplexed.

"Because I'll only encourage you."

"I'm waiting for the bad news there."

She laughed. "Well, I guess we all need at least one person to encourage our crazy ideas."

"Well, if I can be one of yours, I'll count myself lucky."

It made her feel good, and she smiled, not knowing what else to say, but still catching the warmth in his big brown eyes when they met hers. She realized she was staring and quickly looked away. "How's the wing?"

"Oh, it's on the mend, I think," he said turning to look at it. "Doesn't do much for my ego to be carried around by ladies, but hopefully, in the next few days it'll be back in working order, and I'll be free to search futilely again."

"Hopefully that won't last forever," Manuka said, feeling the conflicting pull of two very different desires, one hoping he would find his queen and another hoping he never would.

Large white clouds greeted them the following morning, along with a stiff breeze that howled loudly through the log, making it impossible for them to discuss their plans for the crossing. Queen Fireweed ordered them to assemble on the sandy shore.

"Everyone, we're going to have to stay in a tight standard formation, with myself and our guests in the center, and guards on the perimeter. It's likely we'll run into a few gulls, so we'll need to fly as fast as possible."

"Birds cost us nearly all of our foraging party on the way over," Mustard offered. "What if we set up a decoy group to fly ahead to distract them from the rest of us?"

"We can try that," Queen Fireweed said.

"But what concerns me most is this wind," Foxglove added. "The birds are better equipped for dealing with it than we are."

As the three of them continued to debate, Manuka noticed a giant white box bobbing up and down at the edge of the water. It was so large, a line of Builders were boarding it, and, as she looked across the water, she could see another matching white box coming across, parting the water as it did so. They were using them for transport.

"What are you looking at?" Mesquite whispered.

"What if we hitched a ride on that to the other side like the Builders do?" Manuka asked.

Mesquite weighed it. "That's not a bad idea," he admitted. "Maybe there's a place on it where we could hide so they won't notice us?"

"Looks like there's a ledge on the front."

"You should say something," he said, nodding his antennae at Queen Fireweed, Foxglove, and Mustard, who were still deep in discussion.

"I don't know. Sometimes my ideas go wrong. What if a fish attacks us from the water? I don't want to get anyone hurt again," she added, glancing at his injured wing.

"We could get hurt either way. Just because some of your ideas didn't work, doesn't mean none of them will. Go on. Tell them what you think." He gave her a nudge forward that caught the notice of Queen Fireweed.

"What is it?" she asked.

Manuka presented her idea as diplomatically as she could and made sure she mentioned the risk involving the fish.

"It would probably be better than fighting this wind," Mustard said.

Manuka held her breath as she watched the queen ponder the idea, reminding herself that it wasn't up to her to make the decision on how they crossed.

"I agree," Queen Fireweed said. "All right, everyone. You heard what Manuka said. Let's gather on the front of that box and see if it takes us over. If we encounter any trouble, we'll disperse into two swarms, one to serve as decoy, led by Mustard, and another containing our party led by Captain Foxglove."

They flew over, trying to keep inconspicuously low to the water, and gathered as tightly as possible between two protruding ledges at the front of the transport. The one directly above them provided some cover from the gulls that wheeled and screamed in the air high above.

The bees huddled in an anxious quiet. Queen Fireweed was in the direct center, with Manuka and Tupelo on either side of her. The body heat of the bees created a good deal of warmth in contrast to the cool air that was ruffling the fur on top of their heads. Manuka felt a hand grasp hers in a reassuring squeeze; she looked up, and the queen winked at her, a slight smile on her lips.

"I sure hope this works," Foxglove muttered.

They felt a shudder as something rumbled to life deep within the transport and heard the deafening blare of a horn. It surged forward into the water, and a light spray peppered them. Manuka licked her lips. It tasted herbal, as if there were grass far below the waves. The same scent was in the air all around, along with the cries of the birds high above. She hoped again if she couldn't see them, they wouldn't be able to see her and her friends.

Their speed picked up, and they were soon racing across the water.

Suddenly, a large, pale fly with long, translucent wings flew down and attached itself near them under the ledge. It glared down at them with yellow eyes and made odd, "Hmmmmm! Mmmmmm! Hmmm!" sounds. Soon, it was joined by another and another. None of them had any markings at all but exuded a strange, sour smell. Soon more than fifty of them were there. As they encroached on the bees, they continued to angrily "Hmm…mmmmm… Uhhhhmmmm!" at them.

"Get away, weirdo!" Foxglove shouted, trying to swat at one that came especially close.

"They're fish flies," Tupelo said. "This must be their perch."

"Why do they keep making all those strange noises?" Foxglove asked.

"They don't have mouths," Tupelo said.

Mustard and Foxglove quit their places on the left flank of the group and flew over, placing themselves in front of the nearest fish flies. "See this?" Mustard thrust her stinger forward, showing its sharp black tip. "You're about to get the business end of it. Now scram!" she shouted.

With determined frowns on their faces, the fish flies advanced. More of them joined, echoing their predecessors aggressive "Hmmms" and "Uhhmmmmms". They inched in closer, threatening to hem in Mustard and Foxglove on either side. It was clear a fight would erupt any second, forcing the bees to quit their place and fly into the air. Mustard flexed her wings, as she prepared to dive into the throng, when a familiar fluttering greenish shape appeared and picked off a bunch of fish flies before any of them even knew what happened. It was Lilac, of course.

"Yucky-flies-leave-bees-alone," she chattered, knocking ten more flies off the perch.

Mustard and Foxglove backed away and soon all the flies were in the air in a confused swarm. Lilac jumped out of sight and attached herself to an empty spot under the ledge. The caw of the birds immediately followed as they snapped the flies directly out of the air.

The shore was now in view and, soon, they arrived. At Queen Fireweed's command, they stayed put, waiting for the Builder's to get off and the birds to disperse. Finally, they flew in formation to a nearby elm tree with Lilac behind them.

"That was amazing," Mesquite said, grinning at Manuka. The rest of the bees were brushing the spray from their fur, looking both relieved and exhilarated.

Manuka went over to Lilac, who was carefully cleaning her black and white striped tail feathers. "I thought you were killed," she said.

"No-bees-poke-and-hurt-but-not-dead-just-fell," she twittered. "Followed-you-to-hive-saw-you-leave-and-fly-with-bees-dangerous-so-I-follow."

"We're all lucky you did," Manuka said.

Mustard approached and clapped Manuka on the shoulder. "Nice work to the both of you. You got us over safe and sound."

Manuka felt herself blush. "I don't know. You, Foxglove, and Lilac were the ones that got us over. Still, I'm glad something finally worked," she said.

Mustard turned in Lilac's direction. "Thank YOU, especially, for all your HELP!" she shouted. "I am very glad to see you are ALL RIGHT! We bees are TRULY indebted to you for all your…"

Alarmed at the noise, Lilac jumped back a few paces. Manuka placed a hand on Mustard's shoulder. "I think she understands you."

Mustard stopped. "Oh yeah? Okay, well, I just wanted to make sure she knows how appreciative we all are."

Lilac gave a few quick nods and then hopped up into a higher branch and began preening her feathers again.

"She gets it," Manuka continued.

"Good. Again, I'm very proud of you," Mustard said softly. "You considered the welfare of others and let the queen decide what was right for the group. If you stay on this path, you could be a great leader one day, maybe even a captain of the guard."

It was the first time Manuka had ever been praised, and it brought tears to her eyes, which she blinked away as fast as she could, not wanting to embarrass herself in front of Mustard. Mustard gave her a smile and then turned on her heel.

Once everyone was dry, they set out again. This time with Mustard leading them, so they could refuel in the nearby clover patch. Lilac landed on a sapling and waited. The area was crowded with insects, as before. While the queen's group waited patiently for their turn to sup, Manuka saw a single bee approach them from the other side. Something about its flight struck her as familiar, and she realized it was Cotton.

"Manuka!" Cotton yelled, waving excitedly and laughing. Manuka leapt up to meet her and soon caught her in a bear hug in mid-flight.

"I can't believe it's you!" Manuka said. "I wasn't sure if I would ever see you again."

Cotton hugged her back. "I have so much to tell you!" They flew down to a nearby lilac bush. "But first, I'm so sorry I left you like that. I was angry, and I didn't know how to talk to you about it…"

"You had a right to be angry," Manuka interrupted. "I've been a terrible friend. But I'm working on that, and I'm going to try to be better. You'll see."

"You are who you are," Cotton said, smiling. "And who you are is great. I've felt lost without you. I'm so glad you're okay."

"I'm glad you are too. I was so worried about you. Did you go back to the hive?"

"I did," Cotton said grimly. "And boy do I have a story for you."

After all the bees had managed to find enough nectar to assuage their hunger, they gathered in the branches of a nearby pine tree to rest. Once there, Queen Fireweed asked Cotton to tell them her story. Manuka sat next to Tupelo, and Mesquite sat further way from the group on a smaller branch, cleaning his antennae. He had been oddly distant ever since Cotton returned.

"Is the queen still alive?" Manuka asked Cotton.

"According to rumor, just barely," Cotton replied. "I think Acacia is keeping her alive until she is ready to completely take over. You'll never believe what she's done."

"Try me," Queen Fireweed said.

"I'll do my best." Cotton turned back to Manuka. "Originally, when I left you, I thought I could beg Acacia's forgiveness, but as I got closer to the hive, I realized just how dumb that idea was. Clearly, she would nab me the moment she or one of her guards recognized me. So, to disguise myself, I flew into a pom pom bush and covered myself from head to toe in white pollen and then entered the hive, pretending to be a forager. Her own guards, who are now known as Herders, were at the main entrance but didn't recognize me. Once inside, I was able to find a small bunk in a corner of one of the abandoned wards. There are quite a few of them now, due to all the bees that have died since you and I left.

"Luckily, as I later found out, no one but Acacia, Coriander, and those guards that were with us know about our banishment, so I was able to get around as long as I didn't run into any of them.

"As you would expect, the hive is in disarray. There are a few bees who try to keep to the routines of foraging, taking care of the few young that remain, and caring for the sick and dying, but all-in-all it's a disorganized mess, and bees have even started fighting over honey.

"After a few days, I started snooping around at night. One evening, around midnight or so, I sneaked into the Restricted Ward, where she banished us. The area is now filled with separately spaced cages, all housing wasps. There must have been at least fifty, all terrifying as can be. Acacia came with Coriander, who is now Herder Captain and seems to be her second-in-command, and I hid behind an old nectar pod. Laurel was with them as well, and she and Acacia seemed to be arguing. Laurel asked why Acacia was rearing wasps, but Acacia said they were for claiming new territory or something. It was hard to hear. After that they both disappeared down a narrow corridor where I couldn't follow. I thought she was mean before, but now I realize she is totally insane.

"Bad-bee-Bad-bee-Bad-BEE!" Lilac chirped from her perch above them, stomping her talon for effect. All the bees jumped at once and stared up at her with gaping mouths. Manuka stifled a giggle with her hand.

"Anyway, after that, I knew I had try to find you again," Cotton continued, suppressing a smile. "I returned to Bombas Grove, but the bumblebees there said you had gone with Mustard over the water. I guess I just got lucky that you were here by the time I arrived."

"Don't worry, Cotton. We'll figure out something. Won't we?" Manuka said, looking at Queen Fireweed.

Queen Fireweed sighed sadly. "She's up to her old tricks, but far worse than I expected. We need to find her."

Foxglove leaned in. "Right. How shall we approach her? I can go on my own and offer to exchange Manuka for a meeting with you."

"But she banished us," Manuka interjected. "Why would she want me back?"

"She won't," Foxglove replied. "It's just an excuse to approach her for a meeting with Queen Fireweed and let her know we know what she's up to at the same time."

"But are you sure she would want to meet with Queen Fireweed at all?" Cotton asked.

"It's her chance to prove me wrong and show me what a big shot she's become," said Queen Fireweed. "She'd never pass that up." She looked at Foxglove. "Take an envoy of twenty guards with you, and we'll plan to meet you back here this afternoon."

Chapter 13

It was surreal watching Acacia receive visitors from Queen Trillium's throne, as if the right had always been hers.

Laurel sat in her customary chair to the left of the dais and watched the proceedings. Only a few weeks ago, the hive had been buzzing along like normal, the bees doing their duty and working toward filling their honey quota by winter.

Sure, the flowers had been harder to find, and all the bees were working double time to keep up, but looking back, Laurel could see the past was clearly better than the present.

Acacia was even wearing a crown now. Appropriately, it was made of intricately faceted amber crystals that looked to be razor-sharp from the way the light glittered and refracted off their edges. It matched beautifully with her luxuriant gown of red rose petals but was dissonant with her sour scowl directed at the fierce-looking black bees that had come to visit their hive.

Laurel glanced back and forth between the parties, who faced one another like almost mirror images.

"You're offering to return my own subject to me in exchange for a meeting with your queen?" Acacia asked. "I should feed you to my wasps now for such impudence."

"We mean no disrespect," the one named Foxglove asked. "Your mother…"

"She's *not* my mother!" Acacia shrieked, leaning forward, her eyes bulging.

Foxglove seemed stunned and hesitated before continuing. "I'm sorry, your Grace. Queen Fireweed would merely like to parlay with you on another matter. She offers to return Manuka as a courtesy."

Her mother? Laurel thought. Well, at least that explains the resemblance. When Acacia had originally arrived at Queen Trillium's hive all that time ago, she said she was hopelessly lost from an accidental ride in a Builder's four-wheel transport, but now it was evident the story ran much deeper.

Was it as crazy as the story that was playing out here?

Acacia leaned back, eyeing Foxglove suspiciously. "What does she want?"

"I don't know," Foxglove replied, never breaking her gaze. Laurel wondered if Acacia was buying it, but her eyes were veiled again, no longer betraying her emotions. She casually glanced around the room, which was ringed by thirty guards, all carrying spears. "I'm sure we could get it out of you, if we wanted to."

"You could," Foxglove replied calmly. "But then you would risk turning a amiable conversation with Queen Fireweed into a contentious one."

"Amiable," Acacia snorted, with a chuckle. "I doubt we've ever had one of those in our entire history. And if I go, she'll give me Manuka?"

"Just so, your Grace."

Acacia weighed the idea, glancing sideways at Coriander, who stood to her immediate right, holding a spear.

"It's a way to see the strength of their host at least," Coriander offered.

"And you can't do that on your own?" Acacia snapped, glaring at her. "Must I do everything myself?"

Coriander fell silent and dropped her eyes to the floor.

"If you don't come yourself, I can't guarantee Queen Fireweed will return Manuka to you," Foxglove continued.

"Oh, and what will you do with her?" Acacia asked.

Foxglove shrugged. "We'll probably take her back to our hive. She's smart and resourceful, and we can always use bees like that, as you know."

"As I know," Acacia said, smirking. "But when faced with real ingenuity, you cower. Manuka's just strange enough to be interesting but not intelligent enough to be threatening. Oh yes, I know what your hive would see in her."

Smart, Laurel thought. *If Foxglove can convince Acacia that Manuka is valuable to someone else, she'll never let her go.*

"Fine. I need to survey my territory anyway." Acacia stood, smoothing her gown. "Tell Fireweed this meeting better be worth my while, or I might come back with two prisoners instead of one."

Laurel stopped circling her modest room and sat down miserably on her bed and stared at the empty wall. She still had no idea what to do.

It had all seemed so simple in the beginning: A few bees would get sick from the tainted honey, thereby causing Queen Trillium to come to her senses and lead the hive to a safer, more fertile location with more flowers for foraging. Easy and simple.

Instead, Laurel had allowed Acacia to deceive her and hadn't bothered to stand up to her once. Now, the queen was dying and more than half the hive was dead from the poisoned honey.

To make matters worse, Acacia was planning on rearing hundreds more wasps from the queen they kept in the Restricted Ward.

She shook her head. How had she become such a failure? In the early days, she relished planning the foraging activities and building the honey and pollen stores, but as soon as she decided to really *fix* something, she had mucked it up beyond repair. A wave of anguish passed through her and soon she was sobbing, holding her head in her hands.

Eventually, the tears stopped, and she wiped them away, feeling more exhausted than she ever had in her life.

The way she saw it, she had two choices: either stay and watch the hive she loved fall apart right in front of her eyes, or flee it and die out in the wild. At least with the second choice, she would no longer be in a position to help Acacia complete her horrific plan.

She walked toward the door and turned the handle, pulling it open. The outside hallway was deathly quiet, reminding her of that earlier visit with Acacia, where they had discussed Manuka.

The poor little bee was mixed up in this too and had no one to help her. If Laurel was going to die, maybe she could at least try to free Manuka first? Of all the evil she had done and allowed to be done, maybe this one act would prove that she wasn't as bad as Acacia after all.

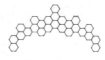

The pine tree's branches where Fireweed and Acacia's parties gathered rustled softly in the late afternoon breeze.

Acacia came armored in a thick breastplate of gold resin inlaid with glittering pieces of amber, forming a circle around her neck. Manuka noted she was also wearing an amber crown as well. It was so sharp, it looked like a weapon. Acacia was joined by Coriander and ten Herders, who gathered above them, each with wasps leashed at the neck. Manuka could hear their hoarse shrieks as they hungrily watched the group below and was relieved she had told Lilac to stay away temporarily – she didn't want the bird's temper getting her hurt.

Fireweed eyed Acacia, her mouth pressed in a thin line. "I see you brought company."

Acacia gave a brittle smile. "Oh, you know me, Mother. I love my pets." She then turned her eyes to Manuka, who stood just behind the queen, next to Tupelo. "I see you brought my own little traitor. I know how you hate to hang on to those. Give her here."

The queen held up a hand. "That can wait. First, we have things to discuss."

"Like what?" Acacia asked incredulously. "You threw me out. I found a new hive. We are finished — *still*. You giving this disgusting little mite further sanctuary only gives me a reason to set my wasps after you — and you don't want that, do you?"

The queen regarded her coolly.

"How does she stay so calm?" Manuka whispered out of the corner of her mouth to Tupelo.

The moth shrugged, her frilly antennae bobbing slightly. "What you see is the true difference between a queen and a worker. Try, for a minute, to imagine yourself the former, not the latter, and you'll understand."

She had a point, Manuka thought.

"If you do that, you won't hear the rest of what I have to say," the queen responded finally.

This seemed to throw Acacia off-guard a bit. "Oh, and what pray tell is that?"

"That I was wrong in throwing you out of our hive as I did. And, moreover, I was wrong for banishing you and Chestnut. I'm sorry."

Acacia looked shocked. "You say this now?" she replied hoarsely.

"It's never too late to admit when you're wrong, no matter what you've done. I should have been more lenient with you both."

Acacia blinked. "Chestnut was…" she began, her voice cracking, and then shook it off. "It doesn't matter. He's gone forever, but *you*, Mother, are still here. And *you* don't deserve my pity or my forgiveness."

"Acacia, listen to me. It's not too late to start a new path. Abandon these wasps. Try to find a way to heal your hive. I don't know what you want, but it can't be this."

"Are you giving me Manuka or not?" Acacia said, biting down on the words.

The queen looked away sadly. "I'm not."

"Of course you aren't. A liar to the very end." Acacia stood, visibly shaking, her fists balled at her sides. "Well, Mother, at least I know what I am. And, I'll tell you something else, once my hive is fully running again, with *my* children and *my* wasps, maybe we'll come calling at your door, and we'll see just how hospitable and forgiving you are then."

She took to the air in a fury, flying straight up into the boughs of the tree. Her attendants followed, with the deafening wup-wup-wup of the ten accompanying wasps. Cotton plugged her ears and turned away at the sound, clearly remembering their escape from their hive that first time.

After they were gone, the group fell into a lull of discontented muttering amongst themselves.

Mustard approached Foxglove. "Do you think she might actually start a war?"

Foxglove shrugged, watching Queen Fireweed, who stood alone, staring into the darkness. "I think if she rears enough wasps, yes."

Cotton came to Manuka's side. "A war between the bees? Since when has that happened? We should be fighting the wasps, not each other."

"I know," Manuka agreed. "We have to find a way to stop her."

From behind them came rustling sounds, and soon Queen Fireweed's guards pushed through a cluster of branches holding Laurel between them and Lilac fluttering behind. "Okay, you two, no need to be so rough. Ow!" Laurel said as she was dragged forward, her robe of sheep's ear leaves catching on the tree's bark. "Manuka! Wait, I need to talk to her. Stop!"

Queen Fireweed turned around at the commotion. "What is this?" she asked, as the guards brought Laurel in front of her.

"Your Grace, the bird caught her spying in one of the high branches."

"Bad-spy! Listening-on-Manuka-friends!" Lilac twittered as she appeared.

Foxglove went to the queen's side. "She is probably one of Acacia's, positioned here to report back on Your Majesty's next move." Then, turning angrily on Laurel, "Well? What did you hear?"

"My name is Laurel. I'm Queen Trillium's second attendant, but I'm not here to help Acacia, I swear. I came to see Manuka."

Manuka and Cotton walked over.

"Is she who she says she is?" asked the queen.

"Yes." Manuka turned to Laurel. "What do you want?"

Laurel looked ashamed. "I've made such a mess of things at home, I figured the least I could do was try to set you free. So I followed Acacia, listened to your meeting, and I was going to wait until dark to try to come to you, but I slipped on a branch, and the bird heard me." She nodded in Lilac's direction. "Looks like I messed that up too. Funny thing, though, you don't look like you need saving after all, so I guess I'm as useless as ever."

"No, I don't need saving," Manuka admitted. "But I doubt you're useless."

"That's right," added Cotton excitedly. "You know the most of anyone about Acacia's plans. You can help by sharing them with Queen Fireweed and the rest of us."

"I'll tell you all her secrets," Laurel agreed. "And to start, you can follow me to the first one."

Chapter 14

The full moon was looming high in the clear night sky when they set out. Laurel flew at the head of the group, flanked on every side by Queen Fireweed's guards, and above by Lilac, in case she exhibited any signs of a double cross. Below them, Manuka heard crickets chirping happily in the dark smudges of brush.

Mesquite flew up alongside her, wobbling tentatively. His wing was operational but still not fully healed, which made his flying somewhat erratic. "Hear all those crickets? They're almost as bad as the cicadas when they get going," he said. "Still, I'm a little jealous of them."

That struck Manuka as odd. "How so?"

"At least they can make noise rubbing their back legs together to find a mate."

Manuka suppressed a laugh. "Have you ever tried it? Maybe it'll work for you too."

Mesquite chuckled. "But I don't want a *cricket* queen."

"Hush, you two." Tupelo was flying just ahead of them and gave them a meaningful look over one of her huge fluffy pink wings. They both fell silent. Manuka wondered why Tupelo still chose to remain with them but hoped it had something to do with her eventually telling Manuka the whereabouts of the tree.

Soon, they began descending as Laurel led them to a large manicured garden bed situated on the far end of what looked like a complex of Builder's hives, the largest of which had a huge rounded roof made entirely of clear resin that softly reflected the moon's glow. They landed together on a mound of turned-up earth at one of the beds that had a discarded pile of tools nearby.

"Obviously, this area belongs to the Builders," Laurel began. "At first, a few of our bees tried to forage from these flowers, but after they had drunk from them, they all died. When we came here to investigate, we found that." She pointed to a white container lodged in the mud. It had black spidery marks on every side, and a ragged opening at the bottom had spilled its contents, forming a fetid pool. They flew over to see it and immediately covered their noses at the ghastly stench. Lilac recoiled and fluttered anxiously on the perimeter.

"Smells like death," Mustard said, stifling a gag as she turned away.

"Yes," Laurel said sadly. "This is what we used to poison our honey. At first, we just wanted to make a few bees sick, so Queen Trillium would agree to swarm and build a new hive — at least, that was what I wanted. But, it got out of hand."

The fumes were so intense that some of the bees began to sway on their feet.

"Bees-get-away. Away-away!" Lilac squawked, jumping between them and the poison, trying to herd them backward with her flapping wings. Queen Fireweed escorted the group to a nearby oak.

"Does this mean we can't visit any of the flowers the Builders touch?" Manuka asked.

Laurel's brow furrowed. "Maybe. Last year, we would have foraged here. Today, we can't go near them. I personally believe that by putting so many different chemicals on everything, the Builders are affecting the way all the plants interact."

Mustard was still staring down at the white container, the confusion and disgust plain on her face. "You really did this?"

Laurel nodded solemnly. "I'll never forgive myself. I wish there were a way to undo it."

"But there is a way," Manuka said. "We need to find the tree. Its nectar will heal what's left of the hive and the queen too."

"The Manuka Tree?" Foxglove said, shocked. "That's just a story. It isn't *real*."

"How can you say that?" Manuka replied. "Our whole history is based on it. Besides, Tupelo says she knows where one is."

Queen Fireweed turned to Tupelo. "Is this true?"

Tupelo shifted her weight uncomfortably. "A strange bee I met last year certainly believed it was your tree."

"And where is she?" asked the queen.

"Dead. Killed by wasps." Tupelo seemed reluctant to continue.

"Well, spit it out. Tell us what you know," Foxglove said.

Tupelo looked at Manuka and sighed. "My mother and I once lived on the other side of that structure over there, in a small grove of maple trees. We were curious about the building, so we inspected it and found that it was filled with plants and flowers that grew inside even when it was cold outside. We tried to enter but never could because it was locked up tight.

"But on the first warm day in spring, the Builders cracked open a few of the resin walls, probably to let the fresh air in, and my mother and I spied a single bee, who flew out into a nearby elm.

"We followed her and saw as we drew near that she was quite exhausted from her short flight.

"Mother, being a kind soul, offered to help her, but the bee, being trapped inside the structure all alone for a whole year, asked us instead to stay and keep her company while she recovered her breath. She had an odd accent and told us her name was Dahlia.

"She originated from a land that was very far away, farther than any of us could imagine. She told us it was a place of green mountains and lush grasses and nearly endless flowers, but the most priceless flower of all was that of the sacred Manuka Tree, a tree that had its own legend among bees everywhere.

"Dahlia had been guarding it vigilantly one day with a small troop of her fellow bees, in accordance with their tribe's sworn vow to protect the tree at all costs, when a group of Builders suddenly came upon them and began digging madly at its base. Well, of course, Dahlia and her tribeswomen rose up in alarm, attacking the Builders to defend the tree.

"It did little good since the Builders wore nets on their faces and sprayed a toxic mist on the bees, killing them immediately. Those few bees that did manage to sting their assailants also died, sacrificing themselves to fulfill their duty.

"Only Dahlia was left, and she clung to the tree, sobbing in fear as they hacked at it again and again, making its delicate branches convulse with every strike and littering the ground below with the white petals from its beautiful flowers.

"Eventually, they weakened the tree so much that they managed to rip it right out of the earth and pull it through the mud to their flightless transport, where they lashed it, with Dahlia still hugging its trunk.

"As they sped away, Dahlia watched in anguish as the mountainside she loved receded and eventually faded into no more than a series of green hills. Still, she held on, terrified of what they might do to the tree and hoping there would be a chance for her to save it or defend it honorably with her life.

"After many hours, they came to a strange landscape as bare and white as the face of the moon. On its surface sat an immense shining bug with huge silver wings that stretched over the sterile ground. At first, she thought they were going to be fed to it, but then the Builders opened its rear and picked up the tree, bound its base in a bag of moist earth and placed it, along with Dahlia, inside the dark belly of the bug. They closed it up, and Dahlia was plunged into darkness. Then she heard the deafening rumble as the beast woke. The sensation of movement followed, slow at first but then faster and faster, and soon, she could tell they had left the ground.

"As the hours passed, she tried to comfort the tree, telling it she would never leave and would find a way to make it safe again. Eventually, after what was probably a day but seemed like an eternity, they landed, and the Builders removed the tree and placed it on another transport, which they brought here," Tupelo said, gesturing to the resin structure. "They took the tree inside and planted it in a raised bed of its own. Then they left, locking the building as they departed and leaving Dahlia inside all alone.

"She spent the winter that way and watched, with great relief, as the tree began to thrive in its new surroundings. When the Builders opened the resin doors, she took the chance to explore the new world outside, and that's when she met the two of us."

"But none of this proves that it's the Manuka Tree," said Foxglove hotly. "Just because some foreign bee took the trouble to travel with it all over creation doesn't mean it's the tree of our story."

"Dahlia swore it was, and since she gave her life defending it, I choose to believe her," Tupelo replied.

"You said she was killed by wasps?" Queen Fireweed asked.

"Yes," Tupelo answered with a sigh. "When Dahlia was ready to fly back, Mother and I asked if we could accompany her to see the tree for ourselves. She agreed, and we flew together toward the building, but before we could enter, some wasps that had made a new nest under the opening attacked us. Dahlia flew to guard the entrance, but she was immediately stung and killed outright. Mother and I tried to retreat, but there were so many of them. In order to buy time, Mother ordered me to flee and fought them alone. She didn't make it." Tupelo turned away, wiping tears from her eyes.

Manuka went to her and placed a hand on her arm. "I'm so sorry, Tupelo. Your mother died very bravely."

"Yes, she did," Tupelo said.

"I'm sorry as well," Foxglove said. Then, addressing Queen Fireweed, "Your Majesty, it still isn't enough."

"Whether it is or it isn't, it's still worth finding out," said Mustard, placing both hands on her hips. When Foxglove opened her mouth to argue, Mustard raised a finger to quiet her. "You mean to tell me that you don't believe it's even worth a *try* to find out if the tree is real and if it's actually here? Who would pass up such a chance?" She looked around at the puzzled faces of the group as they wondered it themselves. Mustard laughed. "You can count me in, Manuka. Let's go find it."

"Wait a minute," said Queen Fireweed. "Mustard makes a good point, yet I recommend we plan our approach. First, we'll go to Bombas Grove so Tupelo can tell her story in front of Queen Prickly Rose who, I'm sure, would want to hear it as well and decide for herself."

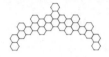

After arriving at Bombas Grove, they gathered all together with the bumblebees in Queen Prickly Rose's Great Chamber inside the rosebush. The room was much smaller and less grand than either the Great Chambers of Queen Trillium or Fireweed, but Manuka noted that, in the usual bumblebee style, it was warm and welcoming.

The bumblebees sat in small circles on the cool earthen floor of the room, with a large wax candle burning in the center of each group, illuminating their faces. Lilac had been given a perch in a small alcove up higher on the wall. She refused to leave Manuka's side after they departed the garden. Queen Prickly Rose sat with Queen Fireweed on a raised mound at the far end of the room. She was as beatific as ever, nodding and smiling broadly at everyone with whom she met eyes. Finally, once it was clear everyone had settled in, she stood and clapped her hands loudly for attention.

"Everyone, as you can see, we have several guests with us here: First, our cousins, the killer bees, led by Queen Fireweed. Also, the esteemed rosy maple moth Tupelo, and Manuka, Cotton, and their friends Lilac and Mesquite have joined us.

"They have brought with them much news. Some of it is very dire, and some of it is extremely exciting. First, many of you have met Manuka and Cotton and know they were banished from their hive. What you don't know is the bee who banished them is an upstart named Acacia, who has poisoned their hive, sickened their mother, Queen Trillium, and begun rearing wasps to boot." Shouts of outrage erupted from the crowd. Queen Prickly Rose waved her hands for silence. "Wasps are our ancient enemies, and we must do all we can to defend our hive and our friends from their scourge. As a result, I propose that we join with Queen Fireweed to restore order at Queen Trillium's hive and stop this abomination from continuing!"

At this, cheers and war cries and much feet stamping ensued.

"Now for the exciting news. Our new friend Tupelo believes she may know where a Manuka Tree grows on this very island!" Surprised gasps followed. "Yet, it is also guarded by a hive of wasps. I believe, as I hope you do too, that we must do all we can to find that tree. Its nectar alone will heal Queen Trillium and her children. If we succeed in doing that, we will certainly triumph in our campaign against Acacia and her foul brood. What say you?"

Deafening hoots and hollers burst from the bumblebees, who leapt to their feet, cheering. Lilac jumped from her perch and fluttered in the air, chirping wildly.

"Excellent! We depart at dawn!"

As the bumblebees dispersed obediently, Manuka and Cotton lingered near the raised mound, where Queen

Prickly Rose, Queen Fireweed, Mustard, Foxglove, and Laurel gathered in a tight throng, undoubtedly planning activities for the following day.

Lilac flew over to Manuka and Cotton. "We-get-magic-nectar-now."

Manuka nodded. "Yes. But you don't have to be a part of that. You've already done too much for us, Lilac."

Lilac dropped down in front of her and cocked her head to the side, her feathered head glittered in the few remaining candles that lit the room. "Manuka-friend. I-always-help."

"Yes, you are our friend but…"

"Manuka-friend!" Lilac chirped impatiently.

Cotton laughed. "And you thought you only had me. Looks like you're stuck."

Manuka smiled. "Okay, Lilac. We'll see you tomorrow when we go to find the nectar."

"Manuka-friend!" Lilac twittered happily and took off. The fur on their heads was still ruffling as she disappeared around the corner of the hive, down the passage that led to the outside.

Manuka brushed the fur out of her eyes and glanced over and saw that the queens, along with Foxglove and Mustard, were still deep in discussion. She frowned, wondering what they were talking about. She felt Cotton's eyes on her, and when she looked over, saw that her friend had a slightly amused expression on her face.

"You're dying to go over there and tell them what you think, aren't you?" she asked.

Manuka blushed. "You can tell?"

Cotton laughed. "Are you kidding? But I'm surprised you haven't done it yet. You're really trying to change, aren't you?"

"Yes, I want to. It's hard, though, having a million ideas and not being able to share them with anyone anymore."

Cotton was about the reply, but Laurel approached them. "I've agreed to return to Queen Trillium's hive to find a way to weaken Acacia internally, but before I go, I wanted to make sure I apologized to you both, not just for what I did to our hive, but also for allowing Acacia to banish you."

"Thanks," Manuka said. "But if I hadn't opened my big mouth and tried to storm Queen Trillium's chambers, it never would have happened."

"Well, you've always done things your way." Laurel smiled.

"Pretty much. But I'm trying to stop that."

"Haven't you ever wondered why you're so different?"

"Plenty of times. But it doesn't really matter, does it?"

"I disagree," Laurel said. "Come walk with me, both of you, and I'll tell you why."

Manuka and Cotton followed her as they exited the bumblebees' Great Chamber and took the main tunnel toward their sleeping area. "About a year and a half ago," Laurel continued, "Queen Trillium decided it was time for her to give birth to a successor who would serve at her side until she died. That successor was you, Manuka."

Manuka halted her. "What? How is that possible?"

"It's true. You were born to be queen after Trillium. And, according to practice, you were placed in a royal pod, and we began to feed you all the nutrients required to aid in your eventual transformation. But, one day, Acacia reported that, somehow, you had missed your feedings for several days. This stunted your growth considerably and made it impossible for you to transform fully into a queen."

"That's terrible," Cotton murmured.

"Queen Trillium was heartbroken, of course. Acacia demanded you be destroyed because you would always be odd, but since you were physically the same as your sisters in every way, right down to the barbed stinger you had when you were born, Trillium refused. Instead, you were placed in a general ward and raised as a simple worker bee. The only thing you kept was the royal name she chose for you — she was adamant about that."

"I don't know why she couldn't just tell me," murmured Manuka. "For so long, I wondered why I never fit in."

"She believed that if you knew, it would make it even more difficult for you to assimilate in such a huge hive. She worried over it a lot, always wondering if it was the right choice."

"Queen Manuka," whispered Cotton. "Who would have thought?"

"Certainly not me," Manuka said.

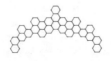

Manuka watched Cotton wave goodbye to Laurel as she walked out into the dark undergrowth of the prickly rose-bush. The funny floaty feeling, as if only part of her was present but another part was somewhere else, had come when Laurel had spilled the news, changing everything Manuka thought she knew about herself.

Cotton was suddenly standing in front of her. "You okay?"

Manuka jumped slightly and heard her own voice say, "Um, yeah."

"Because you don't look okay." Cotton placed a concerned hand on her arm. "Let's go back to our bunks, all right?"

"Okay," she heard herself again and trotted obediently after Cotton as she led the way.

When they arrived, Cotton helped her sit, and she heard her wings crinkle under the weight of her body. She felt her arms and legs go slack and noticed a small, flat pebble lodged in the dirt in the middle of the room. She wondered how it got there; if it had been buried in the dirt for eons before the rabbits had dug the tunnel, or if it had belonged to someone but somehow became separated and lost.

"Manuka, listen to me." Cotton sat down next to her. She felt the bunk squeak, but her gaze was magnetized to the pebble. "Hey." Cotton gave her a nudge. "What's going on in there?"

Manuka shrugged.

"I realize this is a shock," Cotton said. "But I'm really not surprised a bit."

Manuka blinked and turned to her. "You're not?"

"No." Cotton smiled. "You've always been more comfortable telling others what to do than taking orders. Why should it be a surprise that you were supposed to be queen?"

Manuka blinked back tears. "It's not *that*. It's that I'm a freak after all. I belong nowhere. I'm lost, just like that pebble over there." She pointed and then put her head in her hands and sobbed.

"That's not true," Cotton said firmly. "You *do* belong. You may be different, but there's *nothing* wrong with that. You have friends, and you have a place, either here with the bumblebees or with me or with Queen Fireweed. You can choose your own path, Manuka, and that's what's so great about you: You always *have*."

Cotton hugged her close, and soon Manuka's sobs turned to snuffles and finally stopped. She leaned back and wiped the tears from her eyes. "You mean it?"

Cotton laughed. "Of course! Now, we have a big day tomorrow. We've got to get some rest, so you lie down and close your eyes, and I'll do the same. And remember, whoever you are, you're my friend."

Manuka smiled and realized she felt better just know-ing that. She lay down, tried to focus on what Cotton said, and was oddly surprised at just how fast sleep came to claim her.

Chapter 15

Laurel touched down on the polished resin floor of the hive's deserted main entrance. It was just a few hours before dawn, and she was exhausted. Maybe she would grab a little shut-eye before recommending to Acacia that they add a high-protein honey and pollen mixture to the wasps' diet for more energy and stamina. She'd omit the fact that the mixture would be laced with the same poison they had used on the rest of the hive, of course.

She shook her head to clear the cobwebs. She was never very good at lying to begin with and exhaustion wouldn't help. She turned a corner toward the Up Shaft and nearly ran over Coriander, who was leaning against the wall, cleaning her nails with her amber dagger.

"What are you doing here?" Laurel blurted.

Coriander quickly pointed the dagger at Laurel. "What a dumb question from someone who could be asked the exact same thing."

"I was…"

"Out foraging?" Coriander finished, with a downward glance at the scuffed hem of Laurel's robe. "Please. One of our sentries stayed after Acacia departed the meeting with

Queen Trillium and saw them take you prisoner. According to the rest of the report, you've been a busy little bee tonight. Let's go."

"Where are we going?" Laurel asked.

"Where do you think, stupid? To see Queen Acacia."

"Are you sure you want to wake her. I was going to give her a few hours of rest before I gave her my full report."

Coriander laughed. "Is that right? Well, you of all people, know: She hardly ever sleeps."

Laurel was ushered into the Great Chamber, where Acacia was already seated on Trillium's throne, reading a resin. "Your Grace, I'm sorry we've disturbed you," she began. "Coriander insisted…"

"I understand you've been with our enemies all night. What did you tell them?" Acacia said, not looking up.

"Nothing. I…I was trying to learn more about their plans. I was coming straight to you…"

"And what were you doing near the Resin House?"

Laurel was stunned. She hadn't expected to be followed or to have to account for herself so soon. Nothing ever worked out her way.

"Well?" Acacia said, looking up. "Answer or you're going to the Restricted Ward and this will be your last visit. I promise."

"Your Grace, I was trying to gain their confidence. I took them to the garden where we found the poison."

"Where *you* found the poison," Acacia corrected. "You always forget the details. I can't tell if it's because you're an idiot or manipulative or both. Get on with it."

"Well, I showed them the poison so they would tell me their plans."

"And those are?"

"Nothing. They're going back to Queen Fireweed's hive in a few hours."

Acacia stared at her, unmoving. She stood gracefully and swept down from the dais. "So you showed them the poison, and now they're leaving, is that it?"

"Yes, your Grace."

Acacia turned to Coriander. "Does that sound right to you?"

Coriander shook her head, a small smile playing on her lips.

"Isn't it almost feeding time for our wasp queen?" Acacia asked.

Coriander nodded enthusiastically.

"Take her then. If you can't be useful to me, Laurel, at least you can be useful to someone else."

"Wait! No, your Grace. I was only trying to help!" Laurel shouted, as two guards appeared and dragged her away.

"Well, then thank you for your service," Acacia said turning away and walking back up to the throne. After the doors shut and Laurel's shouts could no longer be heard, Coriander approached her.

"Do you want her fed to the queen immediately?"

Acacia raised an eyebrow, considering it. "No, not right away. Maybe she still has some other use. Either that or the extra time will give her a chance to be more forthcoming."

"Yes, your Grace," Coriander said bowing.

"On another note, I've made a decision. Since Fireweed was fool enough to trespass on my territory in the first place, let's settle the score with her once and for all. Better here than when she's at full power back at her hive anyway. After, we can claim her all her territory, including that luscious flower meadow. Gather our wasps and send for my battle armor."

"At once, your Grace!" Coriander said. She turned on her heel and nearly skipped out of the room.

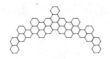

The following morning, Manuka woke with the new knowledge of herself but realized she still felt the same inside. She flung her legs over the side of her bunk and hopped out, standing by herself in the middle of their tiny ward. She heard synchronized noises coming from the main passageway and ran in that direction. When she got there, she saw that all the bumblebees had gathered in their bark armor and were standing proudly in formation, repeatedly stomping their feet in unison twice on the right and once on the left.

Prickly Rose stood at the front of the line and raised her hands high in the air. "Daughters! You are sent forth to seek the tree! Should you find it, you will defend it!"

"AYE!" they shouted. Manuka covered her ears.

"And should you encounter our sworn enemies, you will vanquish them!"

"AYE!"

"Good! Protect one another, our allies, and our hives. Fight honorably and, if you should die, you will feast at the tree with your brothers and sisters for all eternity!"

The bumblebees cheered and began marching out of the hive. Lilac followed them out, zigzagging above their heads, clearly swept up in the excitement.

Cotton and Mesquite approached Manuka together. "Pretty amazing, huh?" Cotton said.

Manuka nodded, feeling a little worried. "I just hope there's actually a tree for us to find."

"It's worth a try. Just like Mustard said." Mesquite smiled. "You ready to follow them?" he asked, nodding toward Queen Fireweed's warriors, who were now filing out behind the bumblebees.

"Yes, but don't you think you should stay here?" Manuka asked.

"No way!" Mesquite said. "I'm going with you. I may not have a stinger, but there's got to be something I can do to help."

What if he gets hurt again? Or worse, what if he's killed?

Manuka felt her chest tighten as it occurred to her she was starting to care about Mesquite just as much as she cared for Cotton. All her life she had wanted friends, but now that she had them, the thought of losing either of them was worse than not having any at all.

"Are you sure you're not needed back at your hive?" she asked.

He looked injured. "You mean you don't want me?"

"No! Not that at all. It's just... I mean... what if you're hurt or captured? It would be all my fault." She looked at Cotton for help.

"I think what she means is: we don't want you hurt for a cause that isn't yours," Cotton offered.

"Forget it. This is the best adventure I'll ever have. You couldn't get rid of me if you tried," he grinned.

Manuka could see it was useless, so she just nodded. "Okay."

"Excellent!" Mesquite said.

Together they followed the last of the bees out into the dappled sunshine.

Manuka considered that everything that would come next would happen because she had managed to convince the bees to search for the tree. In a way, it would be better, and certainly safer, if they all went back to their lives. On the other hand, they would struggle for the rest of the summer to find enough nectar and more bees would die in the winter from starvation. Yet, if they didn't find anything and got hurt in the process, it would still be her fault. Was there any way to avoid bad things happening? She didn't think so. She wondered how Queen Fireweed and Trillium handled these kinds of problems. Probably way better than she did.

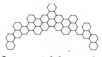

It was a few hours before midday when they drew near the transparent Resin House that held the plants. They massed on a nearby maple tree, where Tupelo advised they would have the best view to plan their approach. Manuka, Cotton, and Mesquite took a spot right behind the elders so they wouldn't be in the way. Lilac was hopping excitedly from branch to branch just above them. Manuka was thinking of telling her to simmer down but then wondered if that was even possible for a hummingbird.

Tupelo addressed Queen Fireweed, who was still dressed in her birch armor, and Queen Prickly Rose, who wore a vest of woven thorns. "See, they've opened one of the resin walls for air," she said, pointing. She had to raise her voice because several cicadas had started whirring noisily in the branches high above. "And right below is the wasp's nest." Manuka squinted and saw a large brown papery nest, huddled just under the opening, which had black and yellow figures pouring in and out.

Queen Fireweed focused on the nest. "We're going to have to use a diversion." She turned to Queen Prickly Rose. "Do you think you could send half your warriors to draw them away? The rest can fight off those that remain, forging a path for a small group to enter and find the tree."

"Yes, I agree," said Queen Prickly Rose, her face solemn, without a trace of its usual mirth.

Soon they were ready, and Mustard gave the command. "First group, you will follow me to lure away the wasps! The second will remain here and follow Queen Fireweed's warriors to defeat those that remain and find the tree!" The bumblebees roared their agreement. (Manuka wondered if her hearing would ever be the same after this adventure.)

She watched Mustard depart and held her breath as they made their way toward the wasps. Then, something caught her attention on the horizon far behind the Builders' hive. It looked like black smoke from a fire, but she couldn't see what might be burning below it. Then, in horror, she recognized what it was: a swarm.

"Look!" she shouted, pointing. Everyone turned.

"It's got to be Acacia," Queen Fireweed said grimly. "Laurel must have told her what we're after."

"But Laurel's on our side," Cotton said.

"Maybe she is, maybe she isn't." Queen Fireweed turned to Queen Prickly Rose. "Either way, we've got to get down there fast to join Mustard. They'll never be able to withstand two hordes."

Queen Prickly Rose immediately turned to those bees that remained. "New plan, everyone! Fly to your sisters NOW! We've got to join with them before Acacia's swarm does!"

The bumblebees leapt off the tree branch, diving down as fast as they could to join Mustard and her group of bees, who was still making their way, unaware of the approaching swarm, toward the wasp's nest.

"This is going to be bad," Manuka said to Cotton and Mesquite. "Come on! We've got to help them!"

"No! You stay here!" Tupelo said, jumping in to block their way with her giant pink wings. "That battle is going to get ugly, and it's no place for you."

"But they're our friends!" Manuka shouted. "We can't just let them die down there!"

"Their path is not yours," Tupelo said firmly.

"Well, we can't just sit here and watch!" Out of the corner of her eye, she saw Lilac still fluttering behind them. "Lilac, can you go and help them?"

"No-stay-here-with-friends!" she argued.

"Please! They need you. We'll be safe up here."

Lilac whirred even faster as she grew agitated, trying to determine what to do next.

"We'll be fine!" Manuka reassured her.

"Ok-I-go! You-stay!" and she was gone in the flick of an eye.

Manuka sucked in a breath, hoping yet again, she had made the right decision.

Tupelo looked up, twitching her frilly antennae back and forth, as she noticed again the cicadas that were still grinding loudly above them. "Maybe there is something more we can do from here," she added. "Come!" She flew straight up in the air, heading for the topmost branches of the tree. Manuka, Cotton, and Mesquite followed.

They reached the upper canopy, and Tupelo stopped to scan the branches and leaves. "She's got to be here somewhere."

"Who?" Manuka said, glancing back down to see that the two bee groups had joined into one swarm far below, with Acacia's swarm closing in.

"Bristlecone, the queen cicada. She has to be nearby with all these males buzzing away."

"I don't get it. What can she do for us?" Cotton asked, looking at Mesquite and Manuka, who looked just as puzzled.

"Bristlecone! It is I, your friend, Tupelo! Please show yourself!"

"Well, you don't need to shout," came a voice from right below them. They turned and saw an elegant dark hand flip over a maple leaf. Underneath, a large black bug with sleepy red eyes smiled at them. "It's good to see you, Tupelo." She came up and stretched large, fibrous, golden wings.

"I'm sorry to disturb you, Your Majesty..." Tupelo began with a deep bow.

"Oh, please. You know I'm not a real queen." Bristlecone stifled a yawn. "They only call me that because I'm old." She hopped up onto the branch where Tupelo stood.

"Of course. I forgot," Tupelo said.

"No matter." Bristlecone waved her away. "What's up?"

"We need your help," Tupelo began. "A battle is brewing far below us, where many bees will die. They're fighting the wasps of the Resin House. I'm here to ask that you send some of your suitors down there to sing. If enough of them go and make enough racket, it'll disorient everyone and stop the battle."

Bristlecone considered it. "I do detest those wasps. They've killed many of my kind this summer, and I'll never forget what they did to your mother."

Tupelo smiled sadly. "She considered you a friend as well."

"Of course, I'll help." Bristlecone flicked her wings together, which made a sharp popping sound, and almost immediately, a group of ten or so male cicadas appeared.

"Move aside, fellas. I saw her first," said one gruffly, taking a few steps closer.

"Forget it, Walnut," said another. "This lucky lady is all mine."

"Hold it, gentlemen," Bristlecone said. "Your ardor is appreciated, but this time, it's my friends who need your assistance, not I."

"Whatever the lady desires," said a third cicada, grinning as he flexed his giant wings showily.

Manuka glanced below and saw that Acacia's swarm had joined with the bumblebees, and another swarm, emanating from the nearby wasp's nest and undoubtedly attracted by the commotion, was also headed in their direction.

Bristlecone then described their task, which was to descend into the center of the fray below, sing as loudly as possible, and discombobulate every insect within earshot.

They agreed, but just before they were about to depart, Manuka interrupted. "Wait, I have an idea." She turned to Cotton and Mesquite. "If Acacia is here with her troops, who's guarding Queen Trillium and the rest of the hive? No one. If you two fly there now, you can move the queen to a new location, somewhere hidden, inside the hive, and I'll bring the tree's nectar to heal her."

"Why not just take her to Bombas Grove?" asked Tupelo.

"Because Queen Trillium was barely strong enough to lift her head the last time I saw her," replied Cotton. Then to Manuka, "What if the tree's not there?"

Manuka knew she had a point. "You're right. There isn't any guarantee, even though my gut says it is. All I know is, it's our duty to protect the queen and our hive. If we pass up even the slightest chance of saving her, how will we live with ourselves, knowing we could have made a difference?"

"Ladies, whatever decision we're going to make, we need to make it fast," Tupelo said.

"You're right," Cotton said. "Where's a safe place we can take her that you'll be able to get to?"

"You have a Drone Ward, right?" asked Mesquite. "Why not take her there? They'd jump at the chance to protect her. We'll tear an opening in one of the exterior walls so Manuka can sneak in. If she has the nectar, we'll give it to the queen. If she doesn't, we'll try to move the queen to Bombas Grove anyway. Sound good?"

Everyone looked at one another and nodded.

Mesquite clapped his hands. "Great! Let's get going." He smiled at Manuka, and she found herself wishing she could hug him — but knew, if she did, she might not be able to let go.

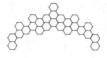

They descended in a ring formation with Manuka and Tupelo in the center. The battle itself was already a writhing dark funnel of screaming and clashing bodies. Manuka wondered how audible the cicadas would be amid the din.

Inside she saw bumblebees clashing with honeybees, honeybees clashing with killer bees, and killer bees clashing with wasps and back the other way around. The wasps shrieked as they grabbed on to any prey within reach and sometimes even each other. Everything was moving so fast it was hard to determine who was who. Suddenly, Mustard came into view. She and another killer bee were wrestling with a particularly large brown wasp. In a shrewd move, they flew behind it and folded its wings, causing it to plummet down further into the fray. When Manuka looked back, they had both disappeared, likely drawn into other scuffles.

A flash of green feathers on the far edge of the mass gave Lilac away, who was zipping in and out, flinging struggling wasps to the earth below with her beak and talons.

"Lilac!" Manuka screamed, waving her hands frantically, but with all the commotion and confusion, the bird couldn't hear or see her.

But a giant wasp close by did and dove at she and Tupelo. They dodged out of the way in the nick of time, and one of the male cicadas jumped in and stomped on its head, stunning it, and it too fell to the ground.

"We have to do this, or we're all in danger," Manuka said to Tupelo.

"Make the ground shake, gentlemen!" shouted Tupelo. The cicadas stationed themselves in a vertical line up and down the sides of the funnel, and Tupelo and Manuka backed away out of the fray.

At first their song was just a low hum, but it quickly became a buzz. Manuka watched anxiously for any sign of the bees and wasps reacting, but the furious fighting kept on unabated. Now the buzz was becoming a high-pitched whir, and she began to feel its vibrations in her abdomen. She thought she saw the sides of the funnel flutter but couldn't be sure. The whir was becoming a scream, and now she could see the sides of the funnel fluctuate. A few of the bees and wasps dropped in a daze to the ground below. The scream got even louder, and Manuka could now feel her teeth rattling in her mouth. Tupelo nudged her, and although she couldn't hear her shout, she read her lips when she said, "It's working!"

It was almost too much to bear now, and she and Tupelo backed off even further so they wouldn't go completely deaf or be overwhelmed themselves. Bees and wasps were now hitting the ground by the dozens, and those that weren't overwhelmed by the noise were being scattered in all directions, unable to keep their equilibrium with the decibels the cicadas were generating.

The screaming kept on until every bee was gone except for a few disoriented flutterers that bobbed in the air, then, finally, the song stopped all at once. Lilac, Mustard and the others were nowhere to be seen. Manuka couldn't be sure if they had flown off or if they were somewhere on the grass below with all the other flailing insects.

It was quieter now, but Tupelo still shouted in temporary deafness. "I guess they took me literally!" She wiggled a finger in her ear.

The male cicada named Walnut turned to them and gave a cavalier salute, indicating that their mission was complete. Manuka watched them ascend together back up to Bristlecone and turned to Tupelo. "Now, we've got to find that tree!"

"Should we stay here and search for the others?" Tupelo asked.

Manuka shook her head sadly. "No time. They did their job, now we have to do ours."

"Right," Tupelo nodded. "Let's go."

They drew near the Resin House and saw that the wasp hive was nearly empty, with only a few remaining guards for the main entrance. To avoid detection, they flew up high over it and landed on the wall of the house. Slowly and quietly, they crawled in through the opening that led to its interior.

Inside, they landed on a small palm tree to regroup. The space was virtually packed with vegetation. Trees, bushes, ferns, shrubs, and endless other plants were growing and competing for space inside raised beds made of stone. The air was warm and filled with moisture. It reminded Manuka of that day, which now seemed so long ago, in her own hive when she'd stolen an extra honey ration during cleanup duty.

"Did Dahlia say what the tree looked like?" Manuka asked.

"No, not really. She said it had small white flowers on its branches and a very unique fragrance."

Manuka couldn't believe she hadn't considered this sooner. "How on earth are we going to find it quickly?"

Suddenly, Mustard flew up and joined them. "I realize you two are trying to find the tree…"

"Mustard! I'm so glad you're alive!" Manuka grabbed her in a bear hug and simultaneously managed to get a mouthful of fur.

Mustard hugged her back. "I'm glad to be alive too and glad I can still hear. Was nearly knocked senseless by those cicadas. Anyway, I really need you both to come with me."

Manuka pulled back. "Why? We're here now. And where is Lilac?"

"No idea but Fireweed's been captured."

"By Acacia?" Tupelo asked.

"Yes. We need to regroup and try to intercept her somehow, before she gets back to her hive. I've already sent a detail of warriors, but I don't want our resources divided in a million directions."

Manuka focused on containing her frustration. "You said the other day you wanted to find the tree. So let's find it."

Mustard threw up her arms. "That was before today's chaos. Had I known that we would have had to deal with two swarms, not one, we'd be in here already looking for it. But now, with a queen missing and a good deal of our warriors either dead, injured, or completely disoriented, we've got other priorities."

Manuka decided to try another approach. "Okay, you're right." Mustard blinked in surprise. "We don't have time to search for the tree now."

"I can show you where it is, if you want," said a high-pitched voice with a lilting accent. A bee, who was smaller and yellow from head to toe, dropped down in front of them.

"Dahlia!" Tupelo exclaimed. "I thought you were dead."

"Nearly." Dahlia smiled. "I got stung in the arm by one of the wasps, but I was able to make it to the tree in time. She healed me, of course." Then she turned to Mustard and Manuka. "If you seek the tree, I can take you to her. I'm sure she would be thrilled to see other bees besides me."

Manuka glanced at Mustard, who sighed in resignation.

Dahlia grinned. "Follow me," she said, and took to the air.

In seconds, they all landed on the edge of a raised stone bed at the far end of the structure. There, in its center, stood a diminutive round bush with delicate branches filled with small shiny green leaves.

"Here she is," said Dahlia, smiling at the tree as if it were family. "I should introduce you. What are your names?"

Manuka didn't know what to say. The tree of her dreams had been immense and majestic. This was just a bush.

"Is that *it*?" Mustard asked. She looked at Dahlia. "I mean, is that all? I expected something, I don't know, bigger."

"You and me both," Manuka said. "Are you sure this is the tree, Dahlia?"

"Of course it is," Dahlia laughed. "The tree in the legend is larger, but reality isn't fantasy, after all."

"Of course not," Mustard murmured, rolling her eyes. "Okay. Let's get on with it."

Everyone identified themselves, but when Manuka gave her name, Dahlia startled in surprise. "You were named after the tree itself?" she asked.

Manuka nodded. "Yes, my mother chose the name." She considered sharing why but thought it might be better for another time.

Dahlia's eyes filled up with tears. "Now I know why I was granted an extra year. You must be the one chosen to take my place."

Manuka hesitated. "Really? I'm not sure…" she began.

Dahlia patted her arm. "First, we must finish the introductions." Dahlia bowed before the tree and motioned to the group to do the same. "Oh, Manuka Tree, we bees are humble and thankful for your love and healing. May I first present to you Tupelo, a wise rosy maple moth, who befriended me a year ago. Second, Mustard, Captain of the Guard to Queen Prickly Rose of Bombas Grove, and finally, a bee that is your very namesake, Manuka. All seek your protection and friendship." She bowed her head to the ground, and the others awkwardly followed suit. After a few seconds, she stood and turned to them. "She is delighted to meet you."

"Um, isn't she supposed to have flowers too?" asked Mustard with a raised eyebrow in Manuka's direction.

"She blooms when she is needed in accordance with the fable," Dahlia replied.

"Okay, we've found the tree," Mustard said. "Although, I admit, I was expecting something else…"

"I couldn't agree more," said a new voice behind them. They turned and saw Acacia standing on the edge of the stone bed, the amber glittering on her resin breastplate.

Mustard looked at Manuka. "Don't tell me."

Manuka nodded. "That's Acacia."

Mustard sighed and turned back. "Fine. I'd tell you to buzz off, but you're too good a trade for Queen Fireweed." She crouched as if preparing to attack but stopped when two giant wasps dropped down, side by side, directly in front of Acacia. Both roared at her savagely, displaying their huge, jagged mandibles.

"Kill them all!" Acacia shouted.

The wasps lunged forward, and Mustard deftly rolled to evade them, then stung the nearest one in its back. It screamed and crumpled to the ground immediately. The other wasp surged toward Dahlia, Tupelo, and Manuka. Tupelo immediately thrust herself in its way, shouting, "Fly!" to the others. The wasp slammed her sideways, making her skid on the ground and disappear over the side of the raised bed. Manuka and Dahlia leapt into the air and were immediately pursued. They attempted to weave in and out of the tree's branches, but the wasp stayed on their tail. Mustard flew up and grabbed onto the wasp's rear leg, but it shook her off. She rallied and landed on its back, attempting to sting, but immediately, it went into a roll, causing Mustard to lose her grip. Just as it leveled out, it inverted and grabbed Mustard, diving for the ground.

"We have to help her!" Manuka shouted.

When Manuka landed, she saw the wasp holding Mustard with both arms pinned behind her back.

Acacia stepped forward, smiling. "When are you going to learn I always win, Manuka?"

"Don't hurt her," Manuka begged. "I'll do whatever you want. You can have whatever you want."

"As if you could stop me from taking it, anyway. This stupid bush might not be worth anything, but at least you'll make a nice snack for my pet here." She nodded to the wasp, and it stung Mustard in the back. She gave out a ragged cry and slumped immediately. The wasp dropped her and began advancing toward Manuka and Dahlia, who had now joined her side. Dahlia placed a hand on Manuka's arm, her eyes never leaving the wasp and Acacia. "I know you'll take good care of the tree, Manuka," she said with a soft smile and then lunged toward the wasp, hitting it with all her might. The impact knocked the wasp back on its heels, giving Dahlia the chance she needed to sting it in the belly. They each screamed in pain as the sting killed them both. Acacia, who was still directly behind, scrambled to get out of the way, but not soon enough. Both the wasp and Dahlia landed on top of her, knocking her unconscious.

Manuka stood still, shocked at the scene that lay before her. Poor Dahlia and the wasp were entwined in a fatal embrace. No bee ever survived the use of their stinger. Acacia looked dead underneath them, but she couldn't be absolutely sure. Mustard lay dead on her right, and Tupelo was nowhere to be found. It was a nightmare. She turned around, tears blurring her vision, and saw the tree, still standing as silently as it had when she arrived. Dahlia believed it to be the true tree, but Manuka wasn't sure now. If there weren't any flowers, there wasn't any nectar to heal. Had it all been for nothing?

"Uggghh…" Came a sound on her right.

She turned and saw Mustard stirring. She ran over. "Mustard! You're alive!"

"Manuka…" Mustard said hoarsely and coughed. Manuka saw she could die at any second.

177

She blooms when she is needed. Dahlia's words came back to her as clear as if she were standing right there. Manuka grabbed Mustard and began dragging her heavy body over to the tree. It took all her might, and every time she gave a pull, Mustard moaned in pain. Finally, she sank to her knees before the tree and bowed, closing her eyes.

In her mind's eye, she conjured the image of the tree in the fable, standing tall and proud in the center of the blooming flower meadow, with thousands upon thousands of bees streaming in and out of its branches. She went all the way in to its center, high up where the trunk split off into the main boughs and found the spot that she imagined the original Manuka would have sat. She was there, old now, and smiling as she watched all the bees thriving happily.

Manuka spoke to her. *I need your help. My friend is hurt. I've been trying to find a way to make things right, but I fail every time I try. I was told this is the tree, your tree. Can you ask her to bloom for me? Please, I'm begging you.*

To her surprise, the original Manuka turned and looked right at her. *You only needed to ask, my dear.*

Manuka then felt a light breeze blow across her back, ruffling her fur, and then she smelled a new scent. It was sweet and tangy, reminding her of a million clover all combined into one blossom. She looked up and saw hundreds of small white flowers opening all at once on the tree. There were more than she could ever count, transforming it into a giant white pom pom.

Mustard gave another weak moan, and Manuka realized she had to act quickly. She flew into the tree and chose a cluster of flowers. Her mouth immediately watered at the rich scent. She thrust her face in the first blossom and lapped up the nectar. It was sweet initially, but then burned as it went down her throat. She took in mouthful after mouthful of liquid fire. Soon, she was full.

She flew back to Mustard, opened her mouth, and gave her some of the liquid. It went down, and Mustard immediately coughed, and her eyes fluttered. *It's working*, Manuka thought. She gave her another dose, and she coughed some more.

"Gods that burns. What is it?" Mustard asked.

Manuka felt tears but smiled. "What do you think?" she said, looking in the direction of the tree.

Mustard flicked her eyes in the same direction and gasped when she saw all the flowers. "Wow…" She tried to sit up to see it better, but Manuka pressed her back down.

"No, you rest for now, and let the nectar do its work."

Manuka heard a scrabbling over at the far end of the bed and saw a bedraggled Tupelo fling an arm over the top and pull herself up. Manuka ran to her. "Are you okay?" she asked.

"Fine," Tupelo said, and then she stopped in awe when she saw the tree.

"She bloomed for us," Manuka said. "Come see Mustard."

They went over together and knelt next to Mustard, who was looking even more alert. Manuka turned to

Tupelo. "I'm going to try to get to the hive with the nectar for Queen Trillium. Can you take care of Mustard?"

"Of course," Tupelo said.

"Good. If I see any of Queen Prickly Rose's bees, I'll send them here to guard the tree."

Manuka was just about to fly off when she heard another rustle and a groan. She turned and saw Acacia dragging herself out from under the wasp. Manuka immediately returned to her friends' side to protect them. Acacia stretched her wings and took to the air.

"As if I would be after you!" she shouted and flew into a grouping of blossoms. Manuka had no idea what the nectar would do for her but knew she didn't have a minute to lose in getting to Queen Trillium.

Mustard stood shakily with Tupelo supporting her and read her mind as their eyes met. "Go!" she shouted. "We'll try to stop her, if we can."

Manuka jumped into the air and flew.

Chapter 16

Manuka's wings were a buzzing blur, and her body felt light as the air. Trees and shrubs zipped by underneath her, the rushing wind roared in her face and through her hair, and water streamed from her eyes. The only drawback was the discomfort inside her stomach, as if pine needles were poking her. She ignored it and pressed on, frantic to get to Queen Trillium and her friends before Acacia could.

She stole a quick glance behind to check but didn't see her. Hopefully Mustard and Tupelo were finding a way to delay her enough to give Manuka the time she needed to get to Trillium.

Out of nowhere, Lilac appeared on her left. "Manuka-fly-fast-now!" she twittered, zipping back and forth, looking at Manuka from alternating angles. "I-try-to-find-you. Where-you-going-now?"

"I'm so glad you're okay!" Manuka shouted. "I've got to go back to my hive to save my queen."

"I-come-with-you!"

Manuka smiled, thinking how having a friend never got old. "It's too dangerous for you, Lilac! I don't want you to get hurt again."

"No–I–help. I–go–with–you. We–find–queen."

"No, I need you to stay away from the hive. Please."

Lilac pondered it for a split-second. "Okay–I–wait–outside. Maybe–find–other–Manuka–friends."

"That's perfect, yes! Go back the way I came. Go into the big Resin House and find my friends. They need you!"

"Okay-okay. I-go-now!" Lilac zipped out of sight, and Manuka breathed a little easier knowing Mustard and Tupelo would have someone coming to their rescue.

Queen Trillium's maple appeared in the far distance, and she pushed her wings to move even faster. In minutes, it was before her, and she slowed to survey the scene. There were a few bees trickling in and out of the hive's main entrance, but they would be easy to avoid. She looped up and around to the back of the hive, where the Drone Ward was located. Mesquite had said he and the drones would cut a small opening for her, and she prayed he had been successful. She didn't see anything right away, but just before she was about to check another section, she spotted a small slit in the hive, just big enough for a bee to wiggle through.

She landed on the papery exterior, crawled toward the opening cautiously, and peered inside. The shaded interior made it hard to see, so she stuck her head in. The place seemed deserted. She entered as quietly as she could and looked around. No one.

A few paces in, she whispered as loudly as she dared, "Mesquite? Cotton?" No answers came. Then, she heard a faint moan that sounded like it was coming from the far end of the ward. She pursued it and found Queen Trillium lying on top of a pallet of dried grass wearing a simple robe of woven spider silk. Her eyes were closed, and she looked incredibly thin and ancient. Manuka was amazed she still breathed at all.

She took Queen Trillium's frail hand in hers and touched her shoulder. "Your Majesty? It's Manuka." The queen moaned again, but her eyes remained closed. Manuka didn't dare shake or move her, so she did the only thing she could and carefully opened the queen's mouth, put her lips to hers, and gave her some of the nectar that was still in her belly. The queen coughed slightly, as Mustard had, and moaned again, but this time it sounded a little stronger.

"That's good, Mother," Manuka said. It was overwhelming being this close to her. "You rest now, and I'll find a way to get you out of here."

"Who's here?" the queen whispered.

"It's Manuka."

The queen opened her eyes slightly. "Manuka... Knew you would come."

The words made her so happy she kissed the queen's hand. "Everything is going to be all right," she said, half to herself.

"Isn't that sweet?" came a voice. Manuka turned and saw Coriander smiling at her, flanked by four guards, each carrying spears. "Seize her!" The guards lunged forward and dragged Manuka from the queen. She struggled, knocking one guard away and nearly overwhelming the others with a sudden new strength, but then a searing pain gripped her, as if she was burning from inside. The flames lapped up into her chest cavity, and she collapsed on the floor, writhing and screaming in agony. She looked up and saw them standing over her. A new spasm came, worse than the previous, and she fainted.

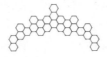

Even though her eyes were closed, Manuka knew they were in the Great Chamber. The number of times the footsteps echoed and the way they reverberated off the ceiling told her that the alcoves high above, where bees would usually fan the room, were empty. She sniffed the air and picked up the scents of Acacia, Laurel, Queen Fireweed, Cotton, Mesquite, and two guards. From their breathing patterns she sensed Laurel and her friends were bound and gagged on the floor next to one another while Queen Trillium was positioned off to the side of the dais, likely in a chair or on another pallet.

Why were her senses so heightened?

"I don't care if she's unconscious, wake her up!" snapped Acacia. Footsteps approached, followed by a painful kick to her back. She sucked in an audible breath and heard Acacia say, "See? Bring her forward!"

Manuka opened her eyes in time to see the floor fall away as two guards hoisted her up.

Acacia was seated on Queen Trillium's throne. She wore a robe made of black petunias and was wearing another crown of sharp, faceted amber that was even more elaborate than the one she had worn to the meeting with Queen Fireweed. Manuka saw that her friends were as she had anticipated, and Queen Trillium was seated in a chair, also bound and gagged, but already looking much more alert. The nectar had to be working.

The guards hastily wrapped Manuka's hands behind her in twine and dragged her forward.

Acacia looked down at her disdainfully. "I should have finished you off when you were just a baby in that pod. Are you ready to end this?"

Manuka considered that just a few weeks ago, she would have found something smart to say, but today, with her friends held prisoner, and nearly everything lost, she could only accept the truth and speak it. "You win, Acacia."

Acacia laughed long and loud. "Is it possible you've changed, Manuka?"

"You haven't. You're just as warped and evil as you were at Queen Fireweed's hive."

"Genius is often misjudged as evil. Do you think Trillium or Fireweed or any one else would have had the guts to turn our biggest threat on itself? All this while, bees have been building hives and foraging to maintain them only to be picked off by predators or poachers. Not only did I invent the spears, I built a weapon no assailant can contest and no other hive will be able to resist. No bee, alive or dead, has achieved as much as I have – not even your namesake."

"Then, if you have everything you want, why can't you let them go? I'll stay."

"Oh, you're staying all right. And you're all dying today, anyway." She stood and began descending the dais toward Queen Trillium. "First, your mother. Then mine." She unbuttoned and removed her robe, dropping it to the floor. Her body was midnight black, and her stinger, which was completely smooth and black, lay shining behind her, like a small tail.

Manuka's vision slowed to a crawl as she watched Acacia approach Trillium. Her own wrists twisted in the bindings. She looked at her mother and thought of all the moments they could have shared together if only she had become a queen as intended. She thought of the tree, how hard she had worked to find it, and Dahlia's sacrifice for her, now useless. What were things of value if they couldn't be protected?

Things of tremendous value require tremendous sacrifice, Tupelo said once.

Sacrifice.

Manuka looked at her mother. She was still weak, but, already, she was looking much better. Given time, she could recover and be able to have more children and lead again.

Her friends, if freed, would have a chance to live.

Tremendous sacrifice.

Instantly, she saw that victory's cost was greater than she could have ever imagined. Persistence wasn't enough, and neither was bravery. It wasn't holding her tongue or thinking her actions through. It wasn't even finding the tree. In the end, she would have to give up the one thing she valued most: her life.

It was the cruelest truth. She might not live to see her mother well again and things put to rights. She wouldn't get to hug Cotton or Mesquite when it was over or thank Queen Fireweed, Mustard, and Tupelo for all their kindness and help. She would have to trust, like Dahlia had, that things would work out, and that vanquishing Acacia would mean something in the end.

She wrenched her wrists apart, feeling the bonds snap behind her, and shoved away each of the guards that held her with every ounce of her strength. They skidded across the floor like twigs, in opposite directions, and Manuka rushed forward, intercepting Acacia just as she reached her mother and roughly shoved her away, unsheathing her own stinger as she did so. With undisguised shock on her face, Acacia stumbled backward, her feet out of sync with her body's momentum, and fell awkwardly on her rear end.

Quickly she scrambled to her feet, a look of total rage, spiced with humiliation, on her face. The two guards had also risen and run to her side. Together they began to advance on Manuka. "Don't!" Acacia screamed, grabbing one of their amber spears for herself. "She's mine!"

"A cheater to the end, huh?" said Manuka, backing away.

"More like a winner," Acacia said, smiling, as she stepped forward brandishing the spear. "You know the legend, yes?"

Manuka nodded, never taking her eyes off Acacia or the spear as the two of them began to circle one another.

"You remember the part when Manuka raises the nectar, and it catches the rays of the sun?"

"It became honey…"

"The so-called ultimate power source," finished Acacia with a chuckle. "But it's actually this," she said, thrusting forward the glittering amber tip of the spear. "That, and the will to use it. I have both."

Manuka lunged forward, grabbed the spear with her right hand and ripped it out of Acacia's weaker grasp. Lightning quick, she flipped it and smashed the butt-end hard across Acacia's temple, knocking her to the ground. Her amber crown toppled off her head and landed with a clatter.

"Not anymore," Manuka replied.

Acacia spluttered and frantically came to her knees, one hand clutching the side of her injured head. "Kill them!" she shrieked at the two guards, who were standing motionless in shock. Only one carried a spear now and hesitated as she looked from Manuka to the queen and back to Manuka.

"What are you waiting for?" Acacia screamed.

Manuka regarded the guard coolly. "You know you don't have to do what she says, don't you? None of us ever have to again."

The guard dropped her spear, and both put their hands in the air.

Acacia stood. "This is far from over," she said and turned on her heel, running for the main doors of the Great Chamber. She flung one open and turned back to them. "Oh, don't worry. I'll be back," she grinned and disappeared.

Manuka turned and grimly walked to her companions. She freed Mesquite first, followed by Cotton, Fireweed, and then Laurel.

After removing her gag, Cotton said to Manuka. "How long do you think we have?"

"Maybe five minutes, maybe less," she replied. Out of the corner of her eye she saw the two guards sneak out the door behind Acacia. She went to her mother, who was still seated and bound, and undid her gag.

"I'm so proud of you," Queen Trillium said, smiling.

Manuka smiled back and went behind her to cut her bonds. "I did what anyone would have done," she replied.

"I'm not so sure about that," her mother said.

Queen Fireweed approached them carrying one of the guard's extra spears. "Can you stand?" she asked. "We need to get moving quickly," she added to Manuka.

"Yes, I think I can," Queen Trillium said, rising shakily to her feet.

"I can help her," Laurel said. She took the queen's arm and put her hand around her waist for support.

"Oh, look at this." Queen Fireweed was staring behind Manuka at her stinger. "Queen Trillium, I think you'd better see this."

"What? What is it?" Manuka said, turning around.

"That's a queen's stinger," Fireweed replied, pointing.

"It's the nectar," Cotton whispered.

"But I'm not a queen. I'm a worker..." Manuka began but was interrupted by a loud bang on the outside of the doors to the Great Chamber.

"That was fast," Cotton said.

Another bang followed, and they heard a familiar roar on the other side.

"I'll bet one of my antennae that's Acacia and her wasps," Fireweed said. She turned to Queen Trillium. "Is there any other way out of here?"

"Yes. Through my chambers, there's a secret passageway leading out of the hive."

"Good. Let's go, everyone." Queen Fireweed stood.

"Wait! We can't just leave!" Manuka shouted. Her friends looked at her as if she were mad. "I mean, what are we supposed to do once we escape?"

"We'll find another place to live," Queen Trillium said. "And eventually, we can build another hive." She still leaned on Laurel's arm, but Manuka knew it was only a matter of time before she would be walking unaided again.

"But this is *our* hive. If we flee, then Acacia has won."

Another loud bang came at the doors, followed by a splintering *crack*.

Queen Fireweed looked exasperated. "Manuka, there's only six of us. We can't fight off the rest of Acacia's wasp horde by ourselves. We've *got* to go."

"Just hear me out a second, okay?" Manuka turned to her mother. "Does the passageway lead to any other parts of the hive?"

"Yes, it goes all the way down the side of the hive, past Confinement, the Drone Ward…"

Manuka turned to Mesquite and Cotton. "Where were all the drones when you got here?"

"Nowhere. Their ward was empty," Cotton said.

"That's because all those who are left were put in Confinement," interrupted Laurel.

"That's great!" Manuka said. "That's where we're going first. We're going to free them, and then we're going to get rid of every single wasp in this hive!"

"What if they won't help us?" Laurel asked. "It's not like we've ever done anything for them."

"If they don't want to help, then at least they can escape with us. But we owe it to ourselves and to them to finally fight for what is ours."

"You're right," Queen Trillium said.

"I agree," said Laurel.

"Me too," Mesquite said, admiration showing plainly in his eyes.

"You know I'm always with you," Cotton said, smiling. She flinched as another bang sounded, followed by more splinters.

"All right," Queen Fireweed said. "Let's get moving, then!"

They ran together toward the queen's private chambers and entered just as the doors smashed open.

Muted morning sunlight filtered through the hive's thin walls and dimly illuminated their path as they shuffled quickly and quietly down the narrow, dusty steps of the queen's private staircase.

As they progressed, it occurred to Manuka that she'd lost all sense of time.

"How long was I passed out after they caught me in the Drone Ward?" she asked Mesquite, who was just ahead of her.

"About half a day, I think. They put us all together in a chamber, and we didn't know what was wrong with you. You jerked and cried out in your sleep a lot. Do you feel different?" he asked curiously.

"Kind of…"

"Because you look a little different."

"How so?" Manuka knew the transformation of her stinger was one thing, but she wondered what else had changed that she hadn't noticed.

"Well, you're taller, for one. Plus, a whole lot stronger, obviously," he chuckled. "And your eyes are, I don't know, older."

"It was definitely the tree's nectar," Cotton murmured from behind them. "It must have brought on your final metamorphosis into a queen."

"Less talking is faster walking," Queen Fireweed said, pointedly.

They all fell silent.

"Here we are," Laurel said. She pulled open the door, and they entered the Confinement Ward.

Immediately, they could smell the bodies and breath of a large number of bees, but, as the light was even dimmer, it took a few minutes for their eyes to fully adjust.

"Hello?" Queen Trillium called. "It is I, your queen."

There was a rustling as well over a hundred bees came to standing in their cages. They went farther in, and Manuka could see that most of them were drones and were very weak and thin. *They must not have been fed in days,* she thought.

"We have come to free you," she said, hearing her own nerves around the edges of her voice. Laurel scurried off in search of the keys to their cells.

After a few moments of silence, a weary voice said, "We thank you, sister." Grunts of agreement followed.

"Fellow drones," interrupted Mesquite, "We are in need of your aid. As you may know, Acacia brought wasps to this hive and poisoned your people. I know you are weak, but will you help us defeat her and her wasps?"

Laurel returned with the keys and immediately began unlocking all the cages. Queen Fireweed and Cotton pulled them open one by one. More drones staggered to their feet. A few still lay on the floor, clearly too weak to move. Manuka felt herself at a loss for words. What could she say that would neutralize their pain? She wanted to cry and tell them how sorry she was that they had been neglected for so long.

Queen Trillium must have felt the same because she was the next to speak: "My sons, you are free to go, and you are free to stay and fight. If you leave, I won't blame you. I am so sorry for making you second-class citizens here. If you can find it in your hearts to stay and dedicate your-selves anew, I solemnly swear you will always be treated with equality, respect, and love from this day forward."

A small, emaciated male drone, who looked older than the others, shuffled forward. "My queen. We have never stopped loving you. Every day that we toiled making spears, we did so out of our love for you and our family."

"Raspberry?" whispered the queen.

The drone smiled sadly. "It's good to see you."

Queen Trillium stepped forward and hugged him. "I've missed you."

He hugged her back. "It's been a long time."

She pulled back and looked at him. "I can't believe I let a little thing like tradition get in the way of our friendship."

"No matter, my queen. We are together now, and that's all that matters. Plus, this is our hive, and we're proud to defend it."

A few claps echoed behind him, followed by more, and soon, the entire ward was stamping and shouting.

"For the hive!" shouted Mesquite, hoisting his spear high in the air, and together, he, Manuka, Queen Trillium, Raspberry, and the rest of the group led the drones out of the ward. Nearby, in the armory, they found a huge cache of spears, lined up against the wall. Each drone grabbed one, and soon they were all gone.

Mesquite managed to organize the drones into four separate groups of roughly fifty each: one led by himself, one by Cotton, another by Queen Fireweed, and the last by Manuka. They agreed that Laurel, Queen Fireweed, and Queen Trillium, who was still improving, would stay with Raspberry and a detail of drones, locked in the safety of Queen Trillium's quarters until the hive was safe again.

Manuka watched each of her friends lead their group out of the armory and prayed they would survive yet another challenge. She felt her mother's cool hand on her arm and turned to her. "This is the part where you trust them to do their duty as you will do yours," she said.

Chapter 17

Everywhere they went, the drones made short work of the wasps they found. In hallways, they rushed forward in tight groups with their spears extended and wedged the wasps into the Down Shafts where they jumped on their heads, knocking them senseless, and then stabbed them between the wings.

It seemed, as makers of the spears, they were the most skilled of all at wielding them. If only they had known this as a hive sooner, Manuka thought.

Either way, any wasp that went up against a drone was a dead wasp. Now faced with a force they couldn't match, the majority of Acacia's remaining Herders surrendered when confronted. They were collected, and all led down to the main entrance where Cotton and her drones had already formed a good-sized corral of Herders and traitor guards near the outer doors.

Once dead, every single wasp was dragged by its black spiny legs past this pen and hurled out over the edge of the hive, where it dropped out of sight. Once the wasps were dispatched, the drones got started on the remaining traitor bees. Most of them begged and pleaded, crying in despair as they were flung over the side. Even though their wings saved them from falling to the ground far below, Manuka knew from experience that their tears were more for the loss of belonging and the shame that came with banishment. Part of her wanted to stop it, but another part of her knew they had willingly made their choices, and the punishment was not only just, but it was what was ultimately best for the hive.

Mesquite and Fireweed returned with their details along with more captured wasps and rogue bees. Slowly, but surely, they were clearing out the hive – but there was still no sign of Acacia.

It's almost too easy, Manuka thought.

"Where could she be?" she turned to Fireweed. "You went all the way up to the honey stores and worked your way down, right?"

"Correct," replied Fireweed.

"What about the Restricted Ward?"

"Where's that?" asked Mesquite.

Cotton groaned. "It's right under Confinement. It's where Acacia was rearing her wasps…" She hesitated as a series of roars erupted from the Down Shaft just behind them. "Oh no."

A swarm of wasps burst from the shaft's opening and filled the room. In the ensuing melee and confusion, the rogue bees broke their confines and joined the battle, outnumbering Manuka and her friends.

Soon a quarter of the bees that fought lay dead on the ground, friends and enemies alike, either killed by stinger or spear. From Manuka's frenzied point of view, it looked like they were slowly gaining the upper hand, but then a new roar erupted. She turned and saw a massive wasp lumber into the space with Acacia riding on its back. She kicked it in the hindquarters and, immediately, it surged toward Manuka.

Manuka leapt into the air and tried to maneuver closer to the ceiling, out of the wasp's reach. Cotton and Mesquite, gathered around its flanks, distracting it with jabs from their spears.

"What's the matter?" called Acacia. "Afraid you can't defeat *this* queen?"

Suddenly a blur of green feathers appeared next to Manuka. "Get-on-get—on-now!" a familiar voice twittered. She jumped on to Lilac's back and held on to her fine feathers as tight as she could. The bird swerved to the left, narrowly avoiding a lunge by the wasp as it reared up on its hind legs. It gave Manuka an idea.

Manuka adjusted her grip on her spear and leaned down to whisper to Lilac. "Now, when I tell you, grab it by the head and pull it up, okay?"

Lilac nodded enthusiastically.

"Okay, now!" Manuka shouted, leaping off her back to the ground, still with the spear in hand. The bird did as commanded and grabbed the wasp, digging her talons into its eyes, blinding it and pulling it until it was nearly standing on its hind legs. The wasp shrieked and lashed, pulling itself free and landing heavily on the ground. The force of the impact caused Acacia to lose her grip and tumble forward in front of it. Manuka thrust her spear with all her might deep into the wasp's shoulder, and it roared and lunged toward her, its jaws gaping. But instead of Manuka, its jagged mandibles closed around Acacia, who was just trying to stand up. She screamed in pain and collapsed as the wasp viciously thrashed its head from side to side. It dropped her in a lifeless and ragged heap on the ground and advanced on Manuka, still tracking her scent.

Suddenly, its torso rose again in the air. Lilac had grabbed it, this time around the neck, and was pulling it upward.

"Now-Manuka! Now-now!" she chirped.

Manuka lunged forward, burying her spear deep in the center of the wasp's exposed abdomen. It gave an ear-splitting shriek and collapsed. Manuka let go of the spear and rolled to her left to avoid being pinned and just made it as she heard the crunch of the beast's body when it hit the floor.

Lilac landed next to Manuka and gave her a quick nudge. "Manuka-alright?"

Manuka nodded and stood. "Thank you, my friend," she said to Lilac, placing a hand on her neck. She caught a glimpse of Acacia's crumpled and ruined body and turned away, her stomach giving a violent heave.

"No-problem. Brought-friends-from-house-too."

Manuka turned and saw Mustard, Tupelo, Foxglove, and a host of arriving bumblebees and killer bees filling the entrance. They immediately spread out and began neutralizing the rest of the wasps, and soon Trillium's drones were dragging away the rogue bees again.

Later, Coriander was found by Cotton and Mesquite and brought forward, kicking and screaming. Her face showed the fury and disbelief of defeat.

"You think this matters? Your hive is *dead*," she spat. "You can't run it with a few sick bees and a bunch of skinny drones."

"Either way, you won't be here to see it," Manuka pulled Coriander's dagger from her belt and tossed it away. "Get her out of my sight," she said. Cotton and Mesquite took her to the entrance opening and shoved her over the side.

Now, with Coriander out of the way, Manuka, her friends, and Lilac gathered together.

"What's left?" asked Cotton. The group looked at one another, but Manuka got the clear sense they were waiting for her to respond.

"After we finish banishing the remainder of Acacia's guards, we should go back to the Great Chamber and put that to rights," she said. Then, turning to Lilac, she added. "Do you think you could stand guard here for a while? We'll keep a contingent of bees with you to help."

Lilac nodded. "Protect-bees."

Manuka turned back to Mesquite and Cotton. "Next, we need to pitch what's left of the poisoned honey and distribute the leftover pollen right away to the drones and any bees who are still alive."

"Good idea," Cotton said. "I'll go up to the stores and see what we've got. We'll bring it all down to the Great Chamber to feed everybody."

"And I'll try to round up all those bees that are left," said Mesquite.

"Perfect," Manuka said.

Chapter 18

Manuka entered through the Great Chamber's cracked main doors and saw that a number of bees had already gathered inside. They turned and stared at her silently, just as they had when Queen Trillium made her address to them during the assembly from so long ago.

Do they still think I'm a freak? she wondered.

Some of them were injured, sporting various bandages and slings. A bee in the middle with an eye patch cracked a smile and began clapping. Soon the others joined in, and now Manuka found she was the one staring awkwardly. They were applauding her?

"Three cheers for Manuka!" the eye-patch bee yelled. The other bees joined in, and soon they were all hooting and hollering.

"Thank you," Manuka said, blushing. "You really don't have to," she added, trying to shush them.

"Never say no to applause," Tupelo said, taking her arm. Mustard and Foxglove were behind her. "Come on. I'll lead you in," and then to the crowd. "Thank you, everyone! Manuka has been summoned by Queen Trillium. She'll see you all again in just a little while."

"What does *that* mean?" Manuka whispered.

"Nothing. Just smile," Tupelo whispered back. "And don't forget to wave."

Manuka did so, and the crowd parted easily in front of them. Together they walked to Queen Trillium's chambers near the dais and entered.

Inside, Manuka saw that Acacia had been laid out on a pallet in the center of the room. She was wrapped again in her black robe of petunia petals and was wearing her amber crown. Queen Fireweed was at her side, her head bowed. "I couldn't just leave her down there," she said as Manuka approached.

"What should we do with her?" Manuka asked.

"I'll take her home with me, and she'll be placed in the royal burial chamber inside our hive," Fireweed replied. "I couldn't make her a queen in life, but maybe it will ease her spirit to rest as one in death."

Queen Trillium stood slowly. "Let's go address the group, ladies. Our bees need us."

Back in the Great Chamber, the room began to steadily fill with more drones returning from their scouting and more bees that had been flushed out of the hive's many remaining Wards. They all looked hungry.

Cotton ran up, looking out of breath, but also excited. "We're throwing out all of the honey, but I found just enough pollen to feed everyone for a couple of days. With the amount of protein and nutrients in it, it should revive us all. Some drones are bringing it down now."

"That's great news, but what do we do when it's gone? Summer's almost over, and what's left of the flowers are going to start dying soon," Laurel said.

"That's why we've got the tree," Manuka responded. "She promised to feed us whenever we need it."

"What do you mean she promised?" Cotton asked quizzically.

"Just trust me," she said. "We'll go there tomorrow night with a small group when the wasps are sleeping. A few drops of her nectar alone will heal everyone, and the honey we'll make from it will certainly be potent enough to last us all winter."

Cotton thought it over for a second. "Let's do it," she said. "We can make a few trips over the next couple weeks and switch up the bees that go."

The room had filled up about halfway, which was more than Manuka had expected. She saw Queen Trillium, who had put on her hexagonal crown, carefully mount the dais at the front, assisted by Raspberry.

"Attention, everyone," she began. "As you all know, it has been a disastrous summer. I hold myself responsible for all that happened, and I am relieved to see so many of my children still alive!

"Also, I would like to take care of something that is long overdue. At my left is Raspberry, your father. According to tradition, he has been sequestered with the drones in their ward but, today, I'm announcing an end to tradition at this hive. From now on our drones will thrive and contribute to our way of life," she turned to Raspberry smiling. "They have been away far too long." At this, cheers from the crowd came. The queen waved them down before continuing. "Now, before I say anything else, where's Manuka?"

Whispers came from the crowd as they all looked around.

"Manuka, please come up here!" Queen Trillium shouted. Manuka approached and mounted the dais. "Manuka, I would like to thank you and your friends for your heroism in saving our hive. We don't deserve you, but I can only hope we'll change that soon enough. I believe you may already know some of this, but I always intended you to be my heir. When your development into a queen was thwarted by Acacia, I was heartbroken. I knew you would grow to be a worker, but I never knew you would save us all and still turn into the queen I hoped you would become."

"But, I'm not a queen…" Manuka interrupted.

"Oh, but you *are*, my dear. Not only did you change physically after drinking the tree's nectar, you proved your-self a queen in every other way you could. You fought for us, healed us. You're more a queen than I was. And now, it's time for you to be crowned." Queen Trillium lifted her own crown from her head and placed it on Manuka's — which she noticed was now level with her own. "With this, I name you Queen Manuka, leader and defender of your hive. May you wear it honorably and fulfill your duties with the same bravery and tenacity you've shown leading up to this day. Now face forward, Queen Manuka, and let your people greet you." She turned her forward, and the crowd cheered. Manuka scanned their smiling faces as her overwhelmed heart pounded in her ears.

"Don't worry, I'm right behind you," Queen Trillium whispered. "Now *smile*."

Manuka did so and gave a little wave, even though a cold sweat had started on the back of her neck. The cheers got much louder and were even peppered with laughter, which made her feel a little better, even though she was still terrified.

How bad could it be? No worse than clean-up duty, right?

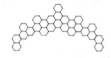

Later that day, after everyone had eaten, Manuka walked to the main exit to bid Queen Fireweed goodbye, who was returning with Foxglove and the killer bees to their hive near the Flower Meadow to supervise what remained of the summer's forage.

"Thank you for everything you've done for us," Manuka said. "About Acacia, I…"

Queen Fireweed held up a hand, interrupting her. "We all choose our path in life. She chose hers, and now you're choosing yours."

"Kind of feels like it chose me," Manuka admitted, itching a spot on her scalp under the crown. Getting used to it was going to take a while.

Queen Fireweed smiled. "I think it was a bit of both. Also, if you ever need a friend, you know where I am."

Manuka grinned. "And you as well. Also, don't forget about the tree. Her nectar is there for you any time you need it."

"Thank you." Queen Fireweed gave her a hug. "Take care of yourself. This hive is lucky to have you." She released her quickly with a smile, then walked to the edge and took flight.

"Maybe we'll make a trip to go see her next summer," said Cotton thoughtfully behind her.

Manuka turned. "We should." She was about to add something, but Mustard and Tupelo joined them.

"Well, I'd say I'm surprised, but somehow, I'm not," she said as she took in Manuka's crown and new appearance.

Manuka hugged her, getting lost in all the fur around her neck again. She pulled back to get some air. "I'm so glad you're all right," she said.

"Me too," agreed Mustard. "That tree's nectar is something else. I brought some back for Queen Prickly Rose. She's at the hive with those who are recovering from the battle, but I'm sure she'll visit here in the next day or so to check on you."

"I may need to visit her before that for her advice on being a queen," Manuka said.

"Yes, but we must sit down together first," interrupted Tupelo, smiling. "So you can tell me the whole story of what happened here."

"It's a long one. Also, I'm sure the rest of the bees around here have their own stories to tell, so you may need to stay for quite a while."

"I'd be happy to. In fact, if it's okay, could I build a nest here in your maple tree?"

Manuka grabbed her in a hug. "That would be fantastic!"

Then Mesquite joined them. "Well, I guess I should be going," he said awkwardly, handing over to her the spear he was carrying.

"What? Why?" Manuka asked.

"I should be getting back to my own hive," he said, not meeting her eyes. "I mean, I've loved every minute being here, but there's really no place for me, you know?"

Manuka looked at Cotton for help. Mustard and Tupelo were silent.

"Surely you can stay another day or so?" Cotton asked.

"Nah, I should get out of your hair. Let you finish getting things in order. Congratulations, Manuka. I'll always be glad to call you a friend." He then turned away abruptly, nearly ran to the entrance's edge, and flew off.

Manuka swallowed hard and turned around, walking shakily back into the hive, not wanting to think about what had just happened. Cotton, Mustard, and Tupelo fell into step alongside her. After a few minutes of weird silence, she tried to think of something queen-like to say. Finally, she turned to Cotton. "A queen needs a chief attendant. Want the job?"

Cotton laughed in surprise. "Me, chief attendant?"

"Yeah. You tell me what to do most of the time anyway," Manuka added.

"All right. But only on the condition that you immediately act on my first recommendation."

"What is it?"

"That you not let a good drone get away."

"What?"

"Mesquite! Go after him!"

Manuka rolled her eyes. "He left!"

"I don't care. Either go after him, or I'm not working with you."

Manuka knew she was right. "Okay, fine! I'm going." She headed toward the main exit.

"I'd say that's a good first step," Manuka overheard Mustard mutter. As she rounded the corner, she saw the area was fairly deserted, except for a few bees that were dumping a comb of poisoned honey outside. Then, a familiar silhouette landed on the edge of the entrance. She recognized it immediately and ran forward.

"Guess that was pretty stupid. Running away from the only eligible queen I've ever found," Mesquite said when she joined him.

"You think?" Manuka laughed.

"Well, here goes." Mesquite fell to one knee and placed his hand over his breast (which she noticed shook a little). "Queen Manuka, I pledge to serve you in all my capacity. Being loyal to only you and accepting any charge you give to me. Will you have me?"

"Since you've already done those things, I'd say I've been your queen for some time now," Manuka replied.

Mesquite looked up at her. "So does that mean 'yes'?"

"I think you should stand, first," she said.

She pulled him back up to standing and looked into his big brown eyes. She was a little taller than him now, especially with her crown, but that was probably all right. She glanced at the spear she still carried. There was a time when she would have given almost anything to possess one but, now that she had it, she realized she didn't need it.

"This is yours from now on," she said, handing it to him.

"Really?" he said.

"Everyone's got to have a job and yours will be protecting this hive – and me."

"You don't really need protecting," he said.

"Sure, I do. And I need bees with crazy ideas, just like you, Mesquite."

He laughed. "Well, I guess we all need someone who believes in our crazy ideas."

"Yes. But we'll make ours happen."

"Together?" he said, grabbing her hand.

"Together," she replied.

Maybe being queen wouldn't be so bad after all, she thought. *Maybe it would be amazing.*

THE END

Acknowledgments

Many people helped this book make its way to your hands. I would especially like to thank:

Mom, for always being just a phone call away with help and encouragement;

Katie, for knowing and reminding me that the toughest adversaries can always be met and bested;

Francesca, for being glad to know there is more to me than meets the eye;

Elena, for boundless enthusiasm and support;

John, for telling me again and again to just do it;

Amy, for holding up a flashlight inside the maze;

Erin, for providing expert insight and advice;

Miranda and Christine, for sifting through my haystack one last time;

Chris, for all those big virtual hugs when times were less than sunny;

Megan, for being my every-day writing friend, always there to dream or laugh;

H.P., for holding me to high standards;

Pat, for helping a stranger with strange requests

Charlotte, for helping me step into the sunshine.

Printed in Canada